Escape by Sea

L.S. LAWRENCE

Holiday House / New York

Library of Congress Cataloging-in-Publication Data
Lawrence, L. S., 1951-
Escape by sea / by L.S. Lawrence. — 1st American ed.
p. cm.
Summary: When the city of Carthage falls to the Romans during the
Punic Wars, Sara, the fifteen-year-old daughter of a Carthaginian senator,
must gather her grief-stricken father and take to the seas, where, with only
a meager cargo to trade, her healing skills, her wits, and her courage,
Sara must face a life wildly different from anything she thought possible.
ISBN 978-0-8234-2217-3 (hardcover)
[1. Survival—Fiction. 2. Sex role—Fiction. 3. Punic War, 2nd, 218-201 B.C.—
Fiction. 4. Sea stories.] I. Title.
PZ7.L4366Es 2009
[Fic]—dc22
2008049495

To Rosemary Beasley, for
medical advice and much else

THE VOYAGES OF THE *HERON*

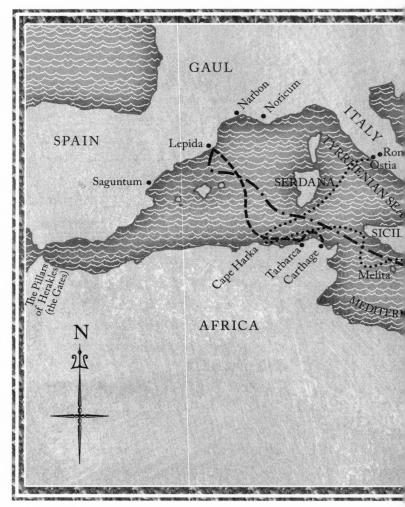

Melita Reach—the strait between Melita (modern Malta) and Sicily
Rietium—about twenty miles northeast of Rome

MACEDONIA

ASIA

NAXOS
CRETE   RHODES

CYPRUS

PALESTINE

Alexandria

EGYPT

Carthage to Lepida
Lepida to Alexandria
Alexandria to Ostia

Escape by Sea

CHAPTER 1

The long African summer was over at last, but the warm afternoons still lingered, humid, ripe as a fruit about to fall. A storm was building, and the heavy air made Sara feel restless and confined. She rose from her loom and walked to the window. Most of the windows overlooked the central courtyard with its cool garden and fountain, but this one faced the harbor. It was the reason she had made a private workroom of this loft at the rear of the big house. When the walls felt too close, she could look out over the blue water, and hear the cry of the gulls, and feel the free wind on her face.

The harbor wasn't busy. The only ship moving was the guard galley. Over the uneasy water Sara could hear the chant of its oarmaster and the answering grunt of the rowers, even the groan of the oars in the tholes. It made a sort of music, a music you could dance to. She had seen dancers, of course. Aram, her elder brother, used to have dinner parties where dancers would perform. Sara had been able to watch them from a screened window—of course she wasn't allowed to actually be there. That would be unladylike.

Sara made a face. Far too many things were unladylike, she thought. But it hardly mattered, in this case. There'd been no dinner parties at all since Aram had gone marching off with the army. Sara missed him, and she was trying not to think about it. The harbor used to provide more distraction, but trade had been quiet for months.

The beat of the oars, the bass rumble, the slow wash of the little waves, and the chant all gave a rhythm. Sara rummaged in her sewing basket and found a pair of thimbles. Clicking them together made something like the sound that finger cymbals made. She checked that the door was closed and listened for a moment. All quiet. She could practice dancing a little, as she sometimes did, but nobody must know.

She removed her mantle and laid it aside, then tucked her skirt up. Leaning back a little, she moved with gliding steps, her arms making smooth, swaying gestures. But the most important thing was to move her hips in the way dancers did, sloping them, rolling them in circles, and making small twitches in time to the music. Sara watched herself in the small hand mirror to see if she were doing it properly. It was difficult to tell. Dancers, it seemed, had hips that moved differently. And you could see what they were doing with them. Dancers wore clothes that showed their rounded bellies.

Sara thought her stomach was rather uninterestingly flat, anyway. It probably wouldn't do for dancing. And the rest wasn't much better, either. Glumly, she peered into the mirror. She was too dark as well, an unbecoming copper color, because of her bad habit of going out into the sun. A Carthaginian beauty should have hair that was either blacker or lighter than Sara's slightly streaky dark brown. The juice of citrons was supposed to help. Her mouth and her nose were both too big, too. But her large brown eyes were quite good. Perhaps she could use kohl to accentuate them....

"Miss! Come quick!"

Sara heard the voice and the urgent footsteps on the stair. She had only just time to readjust her clothes and settle herself into the proper posture of a young lady at her loom before the kitchen boy, Haran, burst in. He was too excited to notice that her mantle was crooked. "Miss, miss. It's Jesapha, miss. This time she's cut herself on the jug she broke. There's blood everywhere, spurting out. She's killed herself, for sure."

One of Jesapha's falling fits, thought Sara. She also knew Haran's love of drama. She picked up her medicine case, which had been her mother's, and followed the boy down the stairs, walking quietly, ignoring him as he danced and prattled.

It wasn't a jug Jesapha had broken as she had fallen but one of the storage jars of oil, fortunately nearly empty. She was still twitching as she lay, and the other servants were, as usual, standing around, making the sign against demons, twittering, and doing nothing useful. Sara walked into the kitchen and shook her head. Her voice cut through the excited chatter.

"Marh, roll Jesapha on her left side and make sure she can breathe. Put this under her head. Now, if you please. No, the demon won't bite you. Abi, sweep up the pieces of the jar and mop up that oil. Use clean cloths, and we can retrieve most of it. Yes, I can see the cut. It's not pumping, so it's not so bad. Haran, get Thamas the gardener. I'll need you and him to lift Jesapha onto the bench here. Keep her on her left side. Marh, if you've finished, get me some strong wine." Sara knelt beside the bench and opened her case. There were silver needles and fine gut thread there. The cut would need stitching.

She washed it out with wine, as Mother had shown her, and used a little clean oil to moisten it so that it wouldn't scar. Then she began to close the cut, one tied-off stitch at a time. It was good that Jesapha had lapsed into unconsciousness. She always did after one of these fits. She would sleep for a few hours and then wake, good as new.

Jesapha was a good cook, despite having the falling sickness, and she was kind. She always had honey in a secret jar, and warm barley bread, in case a hungry child might ask. Mother had told Sara to look after her, and she would have anyway. It had been nearly the last thing Mother had said, on her deathbed, three years before.

Sara finished and rose. Jesapha hadn't stirred, and Sara saw, with a small tug at the heart, that her face had relaxed and become an old woman's, with silver hair spilling out of the head cloth she wore. Sara gathered it back and patted it into place. Jesapha would not like to think that she had been seen like that. She stepped briskly back. "Good. There. She'll do, now. Thamas, you and Haran carry Jesapha to her bed. Now, as to dinner..."

As she finished, she heard the outer gate. "Oh, there's the master now."

Her father, Hanno, had come in from the warehouse. He was calling her.

"Sara?"

"Here," she said, coming out of the kitchen. She crossed the corridor and ran through the inner door into the courtyard.

Father was already in her workroom, looking for her. He turned when he heard her footsteps behind him. "Ah, there you are. I was just..." He looked down and frowned. "Is that blood on your skirt?" he asked.

Sara followed his eye. "I'm afraid so. Jesapha had one of her turns and cut herself when she fell." Father said nothing, but he looked disapproving. "I'll change," she added hurriedly. He nodded, and she rushed off.

When she returned, he was sitting on her weaving stool.

"No ships in today," he said, and shook his head, leaning forward to glance through the window that overlooked the harbor. "Not since *Heron* came in last night. The Romans are keeping close watch. They're trying to strangle the city."

"Ah?" said Sara. She bit down on further comment. She knew about the Roman galleys watching the harbor. She saw their sails sometimes from the top of the house. They'd been coming in closer lately, and of course she noticed everything moving in the harbor. But she couldn't tell Father that she knew it just as well as he did, no matter how much she wanted to.

"Yes. But I can feel a storm brewing. That'll give them something to think about. Drive them off, I shouldn't wonder, probably wreck some of them. They're not seamen, you know."

"A storm?" Sara had been sniffing the gusting breeze all day. "Then I must get the tubs set out for rainwater." In fact, the tubs were placed already and canvas arranged to channel water into them. The African rainy season was short and sudden, and rainwater was valuable.

"It'll be here before dusk, but it'll soon be over."

"It's still quite warm. We could have a late supper in the courtyard once the storm passes, if you'd like. It'll cool the air. The roses are beautiful."

He said nothing. Actually, he wasn't listening. She saw the little line coming and going in the middle of his brow and knew that he was thinking about something else altogether. She folded her hands and waited for him to say what it was.

He frowned, then looked away as though not willing to meet her eye before he spoke: "I thought you'd like to know I've had a message—not from Aram himself, but from the senator who commands his troop. It seems it won't be possible to give Aram leave just yet. There are problems with allowing it at present."

Sara felt cold fingers around her heart. "Aram's well?" she asked. Her brother, Aram, big, cheerful Aram, had gone riding off with the army not a month before.

"Yes, yes, perfectly well. But he's needed. The army needs him. The...Romans have refused terms, and there may be a battle."

Another time Sara might have wondered what word her father had been about to use before *Romans,* but not now. The cold fingers clutched more tightly. Sara found that her own fingers were twisting together. She made them stop.

Father was watching her now. "But there's nothing to worry about, Sara. Our force is far superior, and we have Hannibal to command it. He destroyed every army the Romans sent against him, you know, and that was in Italy and against odds.

The Romans will certainly be routed, they'll make peace, and Aram can come home again. We shall survive. The Romans cannot destroy the city. It's simply not possible."

Sara said nothing. Anything she said would sound as if she were commenting on men's business—the war, or Aram's part in it, or the generalship of Hannibal, or the army, or politics.

Or perhaps she said nothing because there was nothing useful to say. Her fingers were twisting in her lap again, and Father was watching them.

He hastened on. "In fact, we should have some sort of event to welcome him back. An entertainment. Perhaps a reception. I could invite some of the other senators..."

A mumbling of whitebeards, in other words, thought Sara. A starchy affair where there are speeches and everyone is very proper. "Or a dinner party, with Aram's friends," she said with sudden enthusiasm. Aram would enjoy that.

Father seemed uncertain. "Aram's friends? Well, yes, of course, but my dear...they're mostly young men like himself.... I mean, wouldn't you like to be there, too? Although I suppose there's no harm in your being introduced...a few suitable young gentlemen...proper circumstances, of course..."

"Yes. A dinner party," said Sara firmly. "With wine, and music, and entertainers. Dancers, perhaps."

Father blinked. "Um...well, perhaps..."

He broke off. There was the creak of the outer gate and the ring of hoofs on the stable yard. Murmurs. A cry. What now? Sara walked across to the door as footsteps sounded on the stairs, heavy, dragging.

It was Bamas the porter, white as a sheet, his face set in a mask of horror. Staggering, he was supporting a wounded man in muddy, battered armor, bloodstained and scored, the bright metal and the tall crested helmet of the Horse Guard looking foolish now. The soldier was filthy, his eyes bulging, from his head, his beard matted with dirt and blood. It took Sara long seconds to recognize Maro, Aram's groom. He stood quavering on the threshold and fumbled his helmet off, an automatic gesture that opened a half-scabbed cut on his temple. More blood trickled down his face.

"What is it?" asked Father, but he knew already, and Sara could see the dread and the anguish beginning, even as she felt it rising to her own throat. Her hand came to her mouth.

Maro ran a tongue around his salt-lined lips like a lizard. "We are lost," he croaked. "The Romans are coming." He reeled again, and Bamas caught him and propped him up.

"What of my son? What of Aram?" Father had risen. Maro's eyes showed stark white in his blackened face. "Speak!" shouted Hanno.

"Dead," said Maro. "Dead." And he groaned and fell to his knees.

CHAPTER 2

Sara thrust the bundle into the seaman's arms. "And that one," she said, pointing at another package the size of a mule's saddlebags, tied and wrapped in oilskin. "Quickly."

"How much more?" grunted Obala, the captain of *Heron*, Hanno's ship. "We can't be too laden down. We'll have trouble weathering the mole as it is." He was eyeing the ugly, lumpy sea outside the southern harbor entrance and the storm clouds massing in the east. Sara knew he too was thinking about the Roman galleys he would have to outrun.

"Yes," she replied, the unnatural calm still in her voice. She shouldn't sound calm. She wasn't calm. Her hands were shaking, and she wanted to shriek at him, but her voice just went on, dead calm: "I know. But this is the last, and it's only lightweight."

It was peppercorns, cardamom pods, and whole cloves in tight-sewn little calico bags, spices worth well over their weight in gold. "Careful with them," she said, "and don't let them get wet." She sounded like an automaton, said the Sara inside her head, the one with the cutting tongue, the one who must never be allowed out.

Sara remembered the day Mother died. She couldn't afford hysterics then, either. She had wept afterward, when everything had been done and there was time alone. It had become a habit, to put off tears until there was time for them. And now there was no time.

"Father," she said, beckoning to him. He was huddled on a thwart, staring over the transom of the boat toward the crowded wharves. More than crowded. There was a wild throng of people there now, shouting, weeping, gesturing to the ships. Maro had outrun rumor by less than an hour. The whole city knew now. The Romans were coming. "Father," she called again, a little louder.

He turned his head slowly and stared at her. His eyes were empty pits. There was no time for this, either. She wanted to reach out and shake him, slap him. "Come," she said, and stood. The ship's side was a step up.

There had been enough time only to fling necessities into a single chest and to make a hurried selection of the lightest and most precious of the goods in the warehouse. She took all the money she could lay her hands on, the honest silver coins of Carthage prized by every trader in the world, and a few small ingots of gold.

Then to the harbor, through a city that was already stirring, already abuzz. A shore boat had to be hired to carry them out to *Heron*, the fastest of Father's ships, one that had run the Roman gauntlet before and might again. The boatmen knew that something was up, and they demanded twice the usual fare, a bribe that Sara paid without question.

Obala, the captain, had been on deck. Garbled word had already reached him. The ship had not been ready for sea and was only half unloaded after making harbor the day before with three Roman ships in pursuit. Obala had no more than a harbor watch of three men, but he had warped *Heron* out from the pier, ready to take flight, when the shore boat had caught up, carrying the ship's owner and three house slaves— one of them armed and armored. They would be extra hands, at least able to pull on a rope or an oar.

The other servants Sara had sent to the family farms in the hills, with Jesapha being carried in Sara's own sedan chair. The others had promised to look after her, and in return, Sara had freed them.

Lightning flashed. In the rumble of thunder, a few moments later, Sara felt the ragged, hot breath of the wind gust on her cheek. A gale was rising, with the sun getting low as rolling black clouds came up from the east, bringing darkness and the storm. She called down into the shore boat from *Heron*'s deck. "Father! Come now!"

Hanno said nothing. He didn't appear to have heard. Sara glanced toward the docks at the helpless multitude. She could see a glow to the eastern side of the city. A fire had started. The city mob was rioting, no doubt. It would spread.

"We must go," she said, still sounding calm, biting her lip, demanding control of herself. "Thamas, lend a hand here. Help the senator."

They heaved Hanno up over the bulwark and into the ship's waist like a cord of wood. He stood on the deck, blinking about him as if in bewilderment. He had said not a word. But they were here. She had done it. Now there was a chance.

"Father." Something in her desperation penetrated. Slowly he turned to look at her, but there was nothing in his eyes but a terrible remoteness. He did not reply.

She heard the captain shouting orders and knew that there was no more to do for now. She had meant to let the tears come at last now but found they would not. And if they came at all, she thought, they would not be the sort of tears ladies were allowed, a careful covering of the eyes with the hands, a gentle sobbing. No, she could not manage that. If she gave way now, she would scream until her throat was raw. She looked again at her father's face and saw a man she hardly recognized.

The cabin was only tall enough to crouch in. Hanno lay on the shelf against the wall. No, against the deckhead. That was what it was called. And the shelf was a bunk. Sara looked about for a padded mat or something to put on it, but there was nothing.

The urge to scream and beat her fists against the walls was ebbing away, leaving only numb misery. Hanno was simply staring at the roof. And the cabin stank of bilgewater. Once Sara was aware of it, she knew she had to get out. She could not stand this.

She stood, almost without being aware of it, and staggered. The ship was rolling heavily. Thunder rumbled, then cracked like a roof beam splintering. The wind was a steady scream in the rigging, rising in pitch and force. The canvas curtain was flapping wildly, and she reeled to it and pulled it aside, ducking her head under the beam and holding on as the ship wallowed. Spray was gusting across the deck outside, flung with stinging force, and the sky was black. Surely they must be out at sea by now. This couldn't be the harbor, wild with white water, with foam flying like this.

But it was. They were still hauling out. Sara stepped forward, unwilling, fascinated despite herself. The thunder bellowed again, and through it sounded the smash of water on rock and thin wails of distress, like the piping of baby birds against that universal roar. She looked to the left, to port, and there was the outer mole of the harbor, passing slowly. There was a ship driven on it, wrecked, and Sara felt the cold clutch of horror, even through the numbness. She heard the cries. People thrashed in the water. *Heron* was passing them as they drowned.

"No closer. Heave, you sorry bastards! Another cable length and we'll weather it. Heave, gods damn you all!" The captain's voice was rough from shouting.

The men were pulling the long oars called sweeps, with the ship pointing right into the raging wind. Sara looked into the agonized face of the nearest oarsman. It was Thamas the gardener, and he was straining backward, standing on the deck, feet slipping on the planks. Three men were pulling this side, and another three the other. There was Maro, still dazed, and Bamas the porter, struggling with an oar apiece, and the ship's helmsman. Two seamen and the boatman she'd hired were on the other side.

One of the sweeps lay on the deck. There was nobody to pull it, Sara saw. The captain had taken over the tiller. As Sara watched, he tucked the long handle under one arm, deftly hitched a line around the rail, and heaved the coil over the transom. Some poor drowning swimmer might reach it. Then there'd be another body to pull a sweep.

But the shrieking wind was urging the ship toward the rocks that were waiting to tear the hull open. Sara looked and saw swimmers floundering in the waves. The desperate need to escape the Romans was greater even than fear of the storm. People were fleeing in craft that would never live in such a sea. Even as she watched, a small and overloaded harbor boat was swept against the stones and smashed to pieces. A crowd had pressed out onto the end of the mole itself, as if they could find a sort of safety by putting as much distance between them and the Romans as possible.

"Heave!" bellowed the captain, facing the deck, his back to the helpless drowning people, the floating bodies, the wailing groups being swept against the pitiless stones. Other ships were also pulling oars, desperately trying to pass the long mole that protected the harbor. Once beyond, in the open sea, they stood a chance.

Sara saw the oar lying on the deck. Numb, she stepped forward, then halted. Her mouth flattened into a straight line. She turned. "Father," she called. No reaction. She took the few steps to the cot, her head bowed over it. "We're needed," she said flatly.

He stared back at her. Then his eyes shifted, and he looked past her through the open curtain at the deck, at the whitecaps fretting the harbor, at the men straining at the sweeps. He muttered something, almost turning his face from it, but his eyes came back to hers again. Sara stared back, refusing to allow him another retreat. A long moment, then he nodded painfully.

His feet found the deck. He stood, lurching, and then he stumbled forward.

Between an old man and a girl, they could make almost the strength of another rower. It might be enough to edge them around the end of the mole and into the open sea. Sara braced against the sweep and heaved. She had shucked her sandals to give more grip on the slippery deck, and her skirt was torn. The blade dragged through the water, another long, straining stroke. *Heron*'s whole weight was on it, Sara thought. She bent, lifting the blade from the water in time with the others. Her hands hurt. Without surprise she saw that she had already lost skin from her palms. They were too soft. She was too soft for this. She lowered the blade into the water and strained back again, ignoring the pain.

Father was staring aft. Then he frowned and braced again, the slippery oar twisting in his hands. He shook his head, like a man trying to dislodge a fly. Hanno had run away to sea as a boy, because his own father had wanted him given a gentleman's education. He'd been a ship's purser. There must have been times like this back then, in storms or chased by pirates or clawing off a lee shore, when every man shared the grinding labor. This was not the first time Hanno Harcar, senator of Carthage, had pulled a sweep.

She glanced overside. The mole was closer, but they were nearing its head. She saw the problem now. If they could just creep around the end of it, there would be space to set a sail and slant across the breeze, heading out to sea, into the gulf. To do that now would only see them blown onto the rocks. It would be close. Another pair of sweeps, a little slackening of the wind that was pushing them toward the mole, and it would be done.

But the wind was still rising, and they were tiring. The

ship was falling away. On this line, they would strike the mole only ten paces from its end.

The captain's voice came again. "Heave!" And then, "Got you! Gods damn you, puke to leeward." Sara looked up. The captain was picking a wet bundle up by its scruff. It was a wretched little man in an oversize tunic, on his hands and knees on the deck, vomiting up salt water. He must have been hauled in over the stern.

"Get forward!" the captain shouted in the man's ear. "Second sweep, port side. Pull for your mongrel life. Or get back over the side."

He kicked the other forward, and the man went, still retching. Sara had a moment of actual pride. It wasn't their sweep the captain was reinforcing. It was Maro's. Exhausted, wounded, he was nevertheless pulling an oar. She dropped the blade into the water again and braced herself for the next long dragging stroke. It went on. And on.

Finally the captain himself took a sweep. Obala was a powerful man, and he was his own last reserve. He'd tied the tiller, she saw.

"Pick the stroke up," he bawled, and he braced to heave. "Pull!"

It might have been that. Or it might have been her own efforts, or Father's, or the tiny amount that the castaway added. All of them together, perhaps. In a gray mist she saw the head of the mole slip past the side, ten paces away, and through that mist she heard the rough shout, "Hands make sail!."

The mainsail filled. They'd tied it up so that only a third of it showed, but even so the ship heeled far over as the wind caught it. Rain fell in sheets, and the lightning speared again. Sara thought of her rainwater tubs.

"In sweeps. Bring her up," said the captain. "Keep her beam-on to the wind. Course nor'east. Get as far off the coast as you can." He stared out to sea. "Now we've only the god-damned Romans to worry about." Thunder answered him. His face hardly changed. "Sorry, Lord Baal. I didn't mean to slight you. Only I think you're likely to be kinder to us than they would be." He caught sight of Sara, standing by the rail, and Hanno, now slowly looking about him. "Missy. Sir. Get below!" he bellowed.

Sara turned her head. The captain gestured from his place on the afterdeck. She bridled, lifting her chin, squaring her shoulders, looking him in the eye. No! She wouldn't go into that squalid little hutch again. He could bellow as he liked.

He put the tiller into the hands of the regular steersman and pointed to the direction he wanted the ship steered, showing the angle off the wind. Then he swung himself over the rail of the upper deck and walked toward Sara and her father.

"No disrespect, miss, but get below. This is a job for sea-men now. You're only adding topweight and windage and getting in our way." He loomed over her, but she stood her ground, staring up at him wordlessly, defiance in her eye. At that moment, she wouldn't have taken orders from Father, either. Even if he had been capable of giving any. And if not from him, not from this shambling hulk of a sea captain, either.

Obala shook his head, exasperated. "Look, if you really want to be useful, start bailing. She's working her seams, and there's nothing I can do about that. There's the bailing hatches there. Bailing buckets just by. Only get below and let us do our work." Still she glared up at him, her feet planted solidly on the heeling deck, her face set. "Please, miss. We have to work. Please."

The last desperate words, coming from a man who wasn't used to pleading, undermined her. She looked about. Father was still staring, as if seeing the deck, the ship, and the roaring storm for the first time. She turned to him. "Father. The captain says we should bail."

He heard her. He looked down and shook his head again. For a moment she thought he would simply ignore her as before. Then he turned without a word and climbed through the manhole-size main hatch, down into the hold.

Heron had one and a quarter decks, more or less. The first ran the full length of the ship, giving her a hold that was tall enough to stand in. At its bottom was an open latticework of stout, flat battens on which cargo could be lashed down. Below that were only the stones of the ballast. With the ship heeled over like this, water was beginning to pool on the lee side, already ankle-deep in the deepest place amidships. The senator propped a small port open on the side, moving automatically. Sara saw that another was on the other side, the wind side.

He stooped and caught up a pair of waxed canvas scoops, their rims made of a loop of flexible wicker, with another for a handle. He handed one to her. "This way," he muttered. They were the first words he had spoken since the dreadful moment in her workroom. He stooped, leaning against the ship's side. In a single movement he scooped water up from the pool, raised it, and threw it out of the port. It was hard stoop labor. "See. Like this." He gestured. She saw the way of it. With two, they must work in time with each other, one lifting up as the other bent down.

Sara nodded. She was already aching from laboring at the sweep. "Yes, Father," she said, knowing that he would at least hear her now, from whatever far place he had retreated to. They began.

By the time someone else arrived, Sara had descended into a misery of pain and exhaustion. The newcomer was the small man the captain had pulled from the sea. They could take turns then, two working while one stood aside, muscles and joints screaming their outrage. Sara leaned against a pack of cloth, rubbing at her arms and back, trying to release the agony, waiting her turn, while the work went on relentlessly.

"Are you...are you all right?" she asked. The little man had clamped an arm across his belly, like a man with a bleeding wound. His face was a clenched mask, wincing as he bent, but he was scooping and lifting like a machine. As was Father.

"Aye. It hurts a little." The words came in a gasp, but the rhythm never altered. "I think I was banged against a rock or two while I was in the water."

He had a bleeding bruise on his shoulder and probably more bruises or worse under his wet tunic. She stretched out a hand, ignoring her own renewed pain. He waved her away with a half-gesture of the empty bailer as he stooped.

"Should never have gone with the crowd," he mumbled. "Not that I had much choice, once everyone started to run. It was run or be trampled under. They was screaming that the Romans was coming, like they was in the next street or something. I thought I'd get out on the mole, get away from the mob. Lot of others with the same idea. Then I fell off into the water." Bend, scoop, lift, throw. "Or not *fell* so much as was shoved. I know who was doing the shoving, too. Baraka bar-Harlot, the sod. But the next thing I know, I'm being hauled in on that rope, and I've got a ticket out of the city. Baraka didn't mean for that to happen, but fair's fair. I must remember to thank him. I will, too. Right after I kill him." The accent was of the Naq, the city district where ladies did not go. A slave with such an accent would not be suitable as a house servant.

But it had been said in such a matter-of-fact way. "You were pushed off the mole? Why...? Who would...?"

A death's-head grin. "Well, being Baraka, it might have been all in fun, to see if I could swim, like. That'd be his idea of a joke. But I don't think so. See, he owes me money."

Father grunted. He was actually paying attention, watching the castaway's face, weighing up what he was saying. Sara wondered what had caught his attention. "You have to be careful about people like that," she remarked. "Bad debts can be a real problem. Especially when collection is...difficult."

The little man lifted, emptied the pail, bent again. "Oh, Baraka's no trouble, usually, like. He wouldn't normally try something like that, 'cause I got friends. But things are a bit..." He winced, held his side, and gasped.

"Disorganized. At the moment," supplied Hanno, also pausing. He seemed to be groping after a response, seeking meaning. Sara stared in amazement, exhausted and wretched as she was. Normally, Hanno wouldn't have noticed such a person. But this had become a conversation. He gestured with the bailing scoop. "It's the same in my business. They all think the Romans will cancel their debts for them."

The small man looked mournful. "Truth, that. Everyone's a weasel."

Sara shook her head. The world was turned upside down. A senator was conversing with a gutter rat. "The water's less now. I think we can slow down. Father, I'll relieve you." To the other: "And when we're finished here, you come and get some salve for those bruises."

They bailed, each one working until the pain grew too great to bear, each one stepping back in again when another failed. And the senator continued to listen and to reply. Sara, for her part, almost welcomed the grinding ache in her back and thighs, the burning of her hands. Pain was real. Pain took away the other pain. It deadened the mind.

An eternity later, the captain put his head down the central hatch. "Avast bailing now," he called. "Wind's come around, and it's still strengthening. We've put before it, so she'll be working less, and we need to cover the hatches."

CHAPTER 3

Now the ship had her stern to the wind, as if running away from it. She was working less across the seas, her awkward roll transformed into a long, twisting pitch. Steep, short waves followed her, caught her, and broke over her stern-post, wetting the steersman and sometimes washing forward over the upper deck and cascading onto the lower one before being rolled off over the side again.

A seaman gave Sara a boost out of the hatchway. "Like this," he shouted, holding on. "One hand for you, one for the ship. Clap on to the bitts, there. That rack by the mast. That's right. Now you, sir."

"I'm well enough," said Father. And he was, climbing up the ladder and timing his step better than she had, then moving straight to the side, followed by the castaway. He looked around him, one hand gripping one of the ropes that led from the ship's side to the top of the mast. Lightning fizzed and speared behind him.

"Nasty," shouted the seaman in his ear, and Hanno's nod was a real response, too.

"Aye," Hanno, said, and he was actually eyeing the sea and the racing clouds, estimation in his face.

"Think this is the worst of it, though," bawled the seaman. He gestured with his free hand. "Have to cover the hatch."

Hanno shook his head, and water flew from it. It was as if he were trying to clear it. "We'll help you. Sara, hold on tight there."

Between the seaman, Hanno, and the castaway, they got a hatch cover over the opening and lashed it down to eye-bolts on the deck. At least now water washing over the deck wouldn't pour into the hold and swamp them.

The pain in Sara's hands was worse with the salt water stinging her raw palms. She looked at them one at a time. They would need bandages. The ship pitched again, and a wave broke against the stern, sending a sheet of spray flying forward, picked up by the wind.

Hanno was making his way back to her, holding on with one hand, but walking easily enough. She tried to smile at him, a painful stretching of the lips.

"All right?" he asked. Sara nodded. He nodded back, then looked aft.

"Hard from the southeast," he said, his eyes slitted to the flying spray. "Good."

"This is good?" Sara could only stare, aghast. The violent sea and the shrieking sky and the pitching deck seemed insane to her, a whole world that had gone furiously, murderously mad.

Hanno was shaking his head. "It shouldn't last long. These blows never do. But while it lasts, it's carrying us northward, out of the gulf and away from the Romans."

A shout from the upper deck: "A sail! A sail!"

Sara looked, but she couldn't see a sail. For a moment she could see nothing at all, for the ship's stern had risen to block out half the sky. She peered, narrowing her eyes as the pitch reversed, lifting the bow as the stern sank down again.

She shook her head, blinked, and looked again. There was only a long, low thing like a log on the heaving sea, near the ragged horizon. She stared, trying to make sense of it. Lightning showed a flicker of pale tan canvas. There was a sail, after all. It was a ship, like theirs, but longer and leaner.

"*Tremiolia!* Right in the eye of the wind!" The captain waved a hand. He had turned to watch it.

"What is it, Father?" Sara asked. Hanno did not reply, staring aft. For a moment Sara thought he had deserted her again. "Is it the Romans?" She tugged at his sleeve.

He looked down, and she read on his face the struggle to attend, the enforced attention. "More likely their Rhodean mercenaries. They're the ones who use tremiolias. Half galley, half sail, and not much good at either." Grudgingly, "But they're seamen. And there'll be Romans aboard her, nothing surer."

"Will they catch us?" Sara was chilled to the bone, on the ragged edge of exhaustion, trembling, clutching the rail with flayed hands.

Hanno was gathering himself together, letting the sea and the storm and the pursuing ship concentrate his senses and his mind. Watching his face was like slowly focusing her eyes, their blurred vision slowly resolving itself into sharpness and sense.

"Catch us, maybe," he said. "With the wind dead behind, they're faster than us, and we can't come across the wind again, not yet." He nodded out to the right—the starboard side. A flash of something that wasn't a wave came out of the gathering gloom to the east, reflecting the glow of the low sun. Another ship. "I'll bet there's a dozen more of them out there. They've been snapping up anything coming into port for weeks now. We were lucky to have *Heron*. She was fast enough to slip past them on the way in. Maybe she can do it again. And this storm has scattered them."

Sara felt her heart fail. To do so much, to come so far. . . . She leaned her head against her arm and closed her eyes.

Her father's hand gripped her shoulder. "It'll be dark soon, and there's still plenty of wind. If we can just lose this one astern of us . . . well. Let's go and see, anyway."

Sara looked up at him. His whole face had changed. The Romans had to be thanked for that, at least. Something of the young man who had run away to sea was in his eyes again. Almost as if Aram were looking out of them.

No! She couldn't weep now. She would not.

Hanno had stepped up onto the upper deck, the one that covered the stern cabin, and was standing beside the captain. They were talking about something. The Roman ship, no doubt.

Sara scarcely cared. She had little interest in anything now, black exhaustion dragging at her thoughts. They would escape, or they would not.

But at least in the stern cabin she might be out of the wind, and she might be able to bind up her hands. She waited for the roll, then lurched across the deck, ignored the fierce bite of pain as she grabbed the rope that stayed the mast, and then hung on to the rail, heading aft.

She came to the break of the cabin, and she could hear Hanno and the captain. They were shouting at each other, not in anger, but into the wind.

"...can't show more sail. Not yet. In an hour, maybe. She'll only steer wild, going straight downwind, and if we broach-to in this..."

"They're coming up fast."

"Aye. That one's seen us. If we can keep away until dark, we should be able to lose him and slip through the others."

"Edge away west, maybe?"

"Don't think so. I don't know where the land is exactly, but it's not far to the west. I don't want to find it the hard way. Once we're out of the gulf, there's nothing but water between us and Herakles's Pillars." The captain glanced up at the roaring sky. "This storm's a godsend. They can't open their oar ports, not in this sea. And it'll be dark soon." He shook his head. "Well, if they do come alongside, we can make boarding us hard for them."

Sara stared past them, past the break of the quarterdeck. The long black ship was closer, swooping like a hawk on the steep seas. It also was showing a scrap of mainsail, on a mast that was stumpier than theirs. But the ship was clearly bigger, with a higher, narrower stern that rose more easily to the waves. And there were many more people on her deck. Sara's eyes narrowed, staring into the wind. People? Metal glinted. They were armed men.

From behind her came the groan of ropes and the rhythmic grunts of effort. She turned. The crew was hauling stones from the ballast in a net and raising them to the masthead by a rope that led to the top of the mast through a block. The stones would be hurled down onto the enemy's deck as the ship came alongside. Maybe they would crash through it, maybe even put a hole into the hull. She went forward, ready to haul on the rope herself.

But the sailors waved her off. "No need, missy. Go see to your hands," said one. He heaved again in time with the others, and the net of stones rose another foot. "You'd add no weight at all."

Sara glared, but she could see the sense of that. She timed her run, lurched across the deck, and dived into the low opening of the aftercabin, grabbing the batten that did duty as a doorpost, her hand a sudden blaze of pain. She stumbled up against the side. She had linen in the chest.

Actually, there was better. A pair of ladies' leather riding gloves was lying at the bottom. She had no idea that they were there. She hadn't worn them since the last ride with Aram. They had galloped, and he had been laughing. . . .

"Miss?" A tentative voice from the entry. She wiped the back of her hand across her face. Tears or seawater, who would know? The little man was standing in the opening, his arm still tightly held to his side.

She padded her hands, pulled on the gloves, and beckoned to him. A jar of bruisewort ointment was in her medicine case. And yes, once she had that tunic up, she saw bad bruises, scraped cuts, and most likely a cracked rib, one of the lower short ones. No use strapping it, since the dressing would only get soaked and chill him further. She did what she could. A wool tunic would at least keep some warmth in. She found him one and chafed him with a towel so that he was dry when he put it on.

"Thanks, miss. That's easier," he said when she was finished.

Sara doubted that it was, much. "You need a warm bath and then rest." She almost laughed at that. Warmth? Rest?

And as if to underline that, the captain put his head in. "Got a job for you, lad," he said, as if offering a great favor. The little man sighed and went out. Perhaps he was moving a little more easily. Sara repacked her case, staggering as the ship careened about her. She stepped on her torn skirt, swore, and tore the hanging piece off. Too short now, barely knee-length, and ragged. But what did that matter? She used a spare belt and the torn-off piece to make a breechclout under the shortened skirt. The decencies must be preserved. She almost laughed at that, too. When she emerged, the captain was shouting at her patient. "Them stones add a lot of top-weight. She's already rolling too much. It'll have to be the lightest man we've got to haul them out on the yard and drop them when the time comes. You."

"Me? Up there?" He was only a very young man, Sara knew. Barely a youth. She saw his pinched, horror-filled face lift to stare at the masthead where the yard crossed it, far above. "I can't. I . . . just can't."

"Yes, you can, my lad, and you're going to. Hitch him up."

The young man twisted and tried to run but was tackled and slammed to the deck. Sara winced. That would have hurt him again. A seaman cast a loop around his waist and another over his shoulders while he was held down, shouting and squirming.

"No, no! I can't. Heights." His voice rose into a fear-driven shriek. "No, please, you don't understand! I'll spew....I can't..."

They had him in a rope harness, and they hauled him up. His feet left the deck.

"Gods damn and blast you," raved the captain, jumping to one side, then dancing with rage. "Puke on me, you animal, will you? Get him down. I'll have the skin off him—damn me if I don't."

"No use doing that." Sara had heard the blind panic in the young voice, and certainty lent her authority. "You might as well tell him to fly. I'll do it. I'm as light as he is."

"You, miss?" The seamen looked dubious. "You know what you have to do?"

"Yes." She was ready for Hanno's objections. "It's the last place in the ship the Romans will be able to reach. And it's leaning right over the water. The sea, I'm told, is more merciful than Rome."

The senator's mouth had opened. Now it closed again. He slipped his little knife out of his belt sheath. He nodded. "This may be better than either," he said, reversing it to hand it over, hilt first.

Sara took it. Hanno usually used it for cutting open seals on correspondence, but it was sharp and made of good Spanish steel, she knew. Aram had brought it back from the province. She looked down at it, lying in her gloved hand. Father's arm came around her shoulders, hugging her.

She felt the rough scrape of the rope as a loop was dropped

around her shoulders and cinched up under her arms, then another around her waist. The little castaway was pushed aside, and he stood back, looking ashamed.

The captain's voice sounded in her ear. "Now, listen, miss. We'll pull the net up, but you'll have to swing it out. It's no good dropping them stones if you don't put them through that Roman's deck. You'll have to shin out along the yard, as far as you can. Can you do that?"

Sara looked up. The masthead and the yard were describing dizzying figure eights against the racing clouds. She nodded.

"Fend yourself off the mast with your feet. Ready? Haul away, then. Take it smooth, there."

She was lifted off her feet and was instantly hanging from her shoulders and waist by two loops of rope. The ship rolled, and she was swung against the mast, just managing to stop her head from cracking against it. She kicked out, pushing herself off as the rope hauled her steadily upward. The reverse roll took her away from the mast again, but this time she was ready when it swung her back. She propped against it, then gripped it, pushing upward.

Here was the yard, with its sling under her hands. She heard the cry from the deck, and the rope went slack. There was a moment to cling, her thighs across the yard, her arms around the mast. She stared back at the Roman ship.

It was much nearer now. Time was speeding up. She must not be distracted by tears again. She sharpened her gaze. A group of seamen was working by the Roman mast. It looked as if that mast was double, with two uprights instead of one. Sara frowned. What...?

"*Corvus*. It's a *corvus*. Damn him." The captain's bellow reached her. She shook her head, looking at it. He was calling from below: "It's a boarding bridge. It's got a spike on the top end of it like a raven's beak. When they get close enough, they'll drop it on us. The spike will nail it to the deck, and then the Romans will cross two at a time."

There must be twenty Roman soldiers on that ship to one of Carthage, Sara thought. Even so, looking down, she saw that the Carthaginians were clustering on the deck below, and she saw the gleam of blades. Hanno had one, too. But it would all be in vain. If the Romans reached their deck, it was all over. Once their raven-beaked device was firmly fixed, they'd win.

The net of stones hung beside her. There was only one thing to do, and there would be only one chance.

CHAPTER 4

The Roman ship surged up. The sun was a sullen glow on the horizon. The wind was definitely dropping now, and it was already dark. Night was coming. In a little while they would be able to make more sail. The captain had said that they'd walk away from the pursuing Roman ships then. But first, they had to deal with this one.

Sara could see that it was a bigger ship than *Heron*. Perhaps bigger ships did better in high wind. It was sturdier, too, and with a ramming beak at the bow. But it seemed that the Romans didn't intend to ram. They wanted to take, not simply sink.

The captain was shouting orders again, and in response *Heron* was being steered more across the waves. She was rolling more, and suddenly Sara could understand why the captain was doing that. It brought the Romans nearer, but the masthead now leaned far over the side on the roll. And it might make it harder for the Romans to use their boarding bridge, too. She could see what it was now.

It was tied up to the Roman ship's mast, not one plank, but a cross-decking over two long strakes, broad enough for two men abreast. Its beak was a long, wickedly pointed, curved steel spike, just at the top of it. She could see how it would work. When they brought the ship in close enough, they'd let it go. It would fall like a tree toppling. If they timed the roll right, it would slam spike first into the *Heron*'s deck, nailing itself down and forming a pathway that the Romans could charge over. Once they were across, there was no chance of stopping them. They were three to one and properly armed and armored. She could see their mail shirts and shields and helmets.

It would depend on her, then. She would have to leave the mast and climb out along the yard. The Romans were moving in closer. With their bridge, they didn't need to risk an actual collision. That might sink the prey and damage themselves. All they needed was to get close enough.

The masthead leaned as the ship rolled. It would be this side. Sara got one leg on either side of the yard and locked her ankles under it. This was like riding, she told herself. If she could ride a galloping horse, she could ride this.

Now the net full of stones. They were heavy lumps of rock bigger than her head, but one or two still wouldn't be enough. That Roman ship was too sturdy. And the ship wasn't her target, anyway. She knew what the target would be. She hauled the net out along the yard with her, its weight supported by the rope through the block at the top of the mast, but it grew steadily heavier as she pulled it away from the vertical. Now she was far enough out on the yard that on the end of each roll, her feet were over the drop to the sea.

The rope was over her shoulder, cutting into it, the knife in one hand, the other gripping the lashings that bound the yard. The net swung heavily. She could push it out no farther, but this was far enough.

The Romans edged in. They were throwing spears now. She could see the soldiers forming up on the enemy deck, two files of them. When the corvus dropped, they would storm across it. It would all be over in seconds. She must time this perfectly.

The captain could see what she was doing. Hands hauled on the ropes that controlled the angle of the yard. The Romans moved in. Soon. Soon. The seaman at the Roman masthead looked down, watching his own captain. The ships rolled toward each other and away, toward and away. The Roman ship came to the top of the roll, started rolling toward again...

Now! The man's hand flashed down. The rope holding the corvus released and ran through its bolt-hole. For a moment the corvus seemed to hesitate. Then it started to topple, its beak gleaming. It fell with a sudden rush, down on their deck, smashing the flimsy railing and hammering through the decking with a rending crash. *Heron* seemed to shudder, staggering in her roll.

But the bridge was firmly fixed in place. As soon as it fell, the Romans were on it, and they were running across in pairs.

Sara had seen it. She gestured, and the yard swung. Obala knew his business. She was suspended over the corvus now. The first pair of Romans passed below. Another. She had to wait. Not yet. The roll must be at the far point of its swing.

She must release at the right moment, when she was over the middle of the span.

She knew when the moment came. Her knife was sawing at the wet fibers of the net. The roll came to its peak. Now!

The net broke apart. The stones spilled out, a jagged-edged rockfall. One of the Romans looked up, and Sara saw his mouth open, just before the stones smashed him down into sudden bloody rags. His mate dived off the corvus. He might have been trying to reach the side of his ship, but he only bounced off it into the sea. Sara watched him rise for a moment and make a despairing grab, but his armor dragged him under and he disappeared. She felt herself gag in horror. She had done that.

Her aim had been good. The stones had smashed into the bridge between the ships. Into and through it. The planks splintered. One of the strakes underneath split, so that the whole device twisted like a ribbon. The ships rolled away from each other, and suddenly the bridge broke apart with a rending crack. Another Roman fell into the sea and sank like a stone. Sara felt her stomach twist again.

But there were three of them on *Heron*'s deck. Sara had been forced to delay, to wait for the right point in the roll. That had given the Romans time to get some men across.

The fight looked like an eddy in the water of a stream, she thought, looking down on it, her mind oddly glassy-clear, though she was trembling, her stomach a ball of ice. The Romans were its center, fighting back-to-back, the Carthaginian seamen swirling about them. But the Romans were fighters. Soldiers. They knew how to fight like this. They stood like an armored beast, their swords stabbing, a twinkle of light among shadows. The sun was disappearing fast.

She still clung to the yard, trembling, feeling sick. There was nothing she could do about this. One man was down already. Others were giving back, wary of the Roman stabbing blades, unable to pass the large shields. The captain was bellowing something. Father pushed forward. "No!" she cried. He couldn't hear her above the shouting. No. Please. No, not that. Not after...

The sun's last gleam faded. Night had come. They had to make more sail. They could slip away in the darkness if they could finish the fight now.

A blur of movement. A ball hurled itself at the Romans' legs, under one of their shields. Sara's mouth dropped open. A ball? What...?

The ball grew arms and legs, like a spider opening, and it was the little castaway. A gleam of steel showed for an instant, and then one of the Romans folded over slowly, his shield falling to the deck. Another gleam. Another Roman suddenly stumbled, his leg bending under him, collapsing.

The last tried to turn, as if he were going to leap for the side, but there was another gleam, and he, too, fell crashing down on the deck, his helmet coming loose and rolling away. Someone swung a club. A moment later:

"Leave him! All hands make sail. Now! Jump to it, Corda! They're coming in again. Braces. Braces, gods damn you all! Bring her up."

Sara felt the yard swing again. She almost fell from it, her limbs strangely cold and unresponsive, shaking and locked rigid, both at once. She hugged the timber, then forced herself to move along it, shinning back toward the mast like an inchworm on a twig. Sailors on deck were loosing the sail, releasing the lines that held it bunched against the yard. She felt the ship heel, heard the canvas crack as it filled out.

"Another pull on that brace. Heave! Heave, you spavined monkeys!"

From her vantage, Sara could see the Roman ship, though the last light was fading fast. They, too, were making sail, but the sea was still too high for them to open their oar ports, and their ship was heavier. Under the greater sail, *Heron* had shot ahead, clear of their bow. Now she was turning to bring the hard wind on her starboard quarter. She lay over, and the groan of the ropes took on a steadier, more urgent rhythm. The lane of water between the ships began to widen. Now *Heron*'s bow was pointing to the open sea.

The sky was dark now. There was only inky sea and rolling clouds. The Roman sail dimmed and receded into the murk, the fleck of white water at her bow disappearing. In a moment she was no more than a vague smudge on the dark water, just as *Heron* would be to eyes aboard the Roman ship.

"Set the staysail. The wind's dropped enough. Yes, I mean you, Corda. Put your blasted knife away before I show you what to do with it. Gather up them spears. Bring the lady down." He called up to her. "Well done! Nobody could have done better. It's finished now. It's all right."

The darkness closed in. Sara felt the rope harness around her shoulders tighten. She released the yard, forcing her arms to part with it, though they wanted to cling like a baby to its nurse. She was swung through the air to the deck, lowered gently. The ship was rolling less with the sail filled like this. It was far easier to fend herself off the mast.

Her feet touched the deck. She was enfolded into her

father's arms, and there was a moment to do nothing, to know nothing, not to move, not to speak, not to think. Only to shake.

She felt Father tense, then breathe in, and she heard his voice. "Leave him." Then, louder. "Leave him, I tell you. Look at his gear. He's valuable."

And then Obala's, the captain's: "Do as the senator says. Put that knife down, you fool. We might need him. We're not out of this yet. You and you. Truss him up. Do something about that wound before he bleeds to death."

She turned her head.

The last Roman still lay where he had fallen facedown on the deck. Blood streaked his leg. His helmet had come off and was rolling in the angle between the bulwark and the deck. His hair, Sara saw with surprise, was the color of ripe wheat.

Two seamen were just heaving another Roman over the side. Sara found herself hoping that he was already dead. The last one was bleeding, and they were binding his hands, though his head lolled helplessly.

Her father's voice. "Sara. Can you do something about him?"

She looked up at him. Surely he couldn't mean...

But he did. "It's too much, I know," he said. "And most of me wants to let him die, too. But look at him."

Sara did. She realized with a shock that he wasn't much older than she was. The dusty-blond hair was cut short, the nascent beard carefully shaven. His face was pale—that was probably the blood loss—and it made his freckles stand out more. His eyebrows were a little darker than his hair, and he had an arrogant, jutting beak of a nose. And a mouth that quivered, as though still in pain . . .

Her father was speaking again. "See how costly his gear is? That armor's been made for him, and it's fine work—riveted mail, chased leather. His sword has ivory grips. His helmet's engraved. He's a rich man, or a rich man's son. That means a ransom, or maybe he'll make a hostage. Let's not have him die on us."

Gear? Armor? Sara shook her head. What was that to her? This was a Roman. She stared at him as he lay on the deck, and she saw the blood, a thick streak of it in the seawater that washed across the deck. They picked him up, then they looked at her.

"Bring him into the cabin," she heard herself say.

CHAPTER 5

Bring the light closer, Father," Sara said. "Hold it steady."

The sea had fallen a little. With the wind on her quarter, *Heron* was riding more smoothly. Sara's hands worked automatically, her mind feeling empty, drained. It was as if she were someone else watching out of her own eyes. The wound was deep, about three fingers long, high on the outer side of the left thigh. Muscle had been cut. Once she cleaned it and swabbed the welling blood, she could see the fibers. It would need two layers of stitching, once with gut, and care would be required, or it would pucker. Sara bent over it, willing her hands not to shake. The curved silver needle wouldn't thread. She had to pull her mind back, had to make herself pay attention. She summoned up the will, forcing herself to concentrate on what was going on around her. The patient was lying comatose. She would have to see to the head injury next, as soon as she had stanched the blood. Blood matted the fair hair, but at least that was no longer bleeding fresh. She heard conversations on deck, outside the curtain.

"…when you puked on the captain. Lordy, how he danced."

"Couldn't help it. I'm like that with heights, see." The voice was sullen.

"Oh, I could see that, for certain. But nobody can say you haven't got a strong stomach, lad. Don't think I've ever seen a man's gut throw a load so far." Pause. "Oh, put it away. No man's going to call you shy in a fight, not after what you did to them Romans. I know you can use a knife. No need to prove it again."

A mumble. Sara couldn't hear the words. Her hands were steadier. She pulled the thread through. Another tied-off stitch. The wound must be closed neatly, or the scar would be ugly. She glanced at the unconscious pale face, wondering if he felt the pain, and shook her head, concentrating fiercely.

Another voice, a third. "*I* never saw nothing like it, neither. Rolling under their feet like that. They must've thought you was a…a weasel, or something. Well, you bit 'em right in the balls, you did."

"Aye. So don't worry about the other. Pity you're like that about heights, in a way, mind. You're the natural size for a topman."

"Well, we only need one man to go aloft. And we got that." The third man laughed coarsely. "Not a *man*, like. Oh, yes. You could see that she wasn't no man, but—"

"You shut your ugly mouth about her. She saved your hide and mine. You got no right talking like that.…" The Naq accent had thickened, becoming a threat.

Sara pulled the last stitch closed. Now the bandage. The blood loss had slowed to a seeping, and the patient was breathing more deeply. That was a good sign.

A more distant shout—from above, from the quarterdeck. "You apes got nothing else to do? Corda, your watch below. Get your head down. You're on deck again at dawn. You, waterman: Bas, is it? Get them ropes snugged down and coiled. And you, what's your name...?"

"Jerem. My name is Jerem."

Sara, hearing the challenge in the young voice, paused to listen as she slit the end of the bandage and tied it neatly. She wondered how the captain would respond.

"Jerem, is it? All right. You call me *captain*. I'm the one pulled you out of the drink. You was drowning, remember?"

A mumble was the only response.

"I pulled you out, I can throw you back. You doubt me, boy?" Pause. "All right, then. You did well enough. You'll do for steward, for now. Six silvers for the voyage. If you don't like it, you can step over the side anytime you want. There's a bread bag hanging below, and some jugs of olives in the forepeak. And wine and a side of bacon. Serve some food out. Step lively, now."

The Roman's skull was intact. The knock on the head was no more than a concussion. Sara's hands had finished the binding neatly, as usual working by themselves while she thought about other things. "That should do, now," she said. She looked around. "Father, there's another bed on that side. There must be some blankets somewhere...."

Hanno shook his head. "He can sleep on the deck. It won't matter to him for a while, I dare say."

"It's wet. So is he. If we don't get him dry and warm, he'll just get the lung fever and die anyway. It always happens when there's loss of blood like this." She paused. "Not that

I care, Father, but you wanted him saved, and we've been to some trouble over him already. No point in not doing it properly now."

The senator grunted. "Very well. But there's only one other cot." He hesitated.

Sara was really too tired to be amused by her father's dilemma. If the Roman occupied one cot, who would sleep in the other? If it was Sara—which was logical, if she was to doctor him—it would mean that she had a young man in her room. That young man could no more set foot on the deck than he could swim back to Rome, but that was of no importance, of course. If Father took the other cot for himself, Sara would have to sleep outside on deck or in the hold, among the rough sailors. If neither of them, then who? The captain? That would mean that he took the cabin while the ship's owner—a senator to boot—slept in the hold. And his daughter did, too.

Just at the moment, though, Sara didn't particularly care where she slept, as long as she could sleep soon. Even the damp bare boards of the deck looked good, now that seawater was no longer swilling over them. The waves were no longer high enough to break over the stern, and the ship was rolling away from them.

In the end, a compromise was found. Father obtained a piece of heavy canvas from the captain, a strip five cubits long and two wide, double-hemmed and stitched, with a batten sewn into the narrow ends. A hammock, he called it. Apparently it could be hung from hooks on either side of the cabin. He would occupy it, he said. They could both sleep in here. All three, that is. And the Roman could stay tied up.

"But as soon as he's out of danger, he'll be out of here, too," said Father. "The hold's good enough for him."

"Wind's backed; the storm's passing. It's settled north of east, for now. But the season has turned, no doubt about it, and the wind must come west before long."

The sun was rising. The Roman had woken, stared around, mumbled something, and fallen asleep again. Perhaps he would wake up. Perhaps not. That he was still breathing was all Sara knew. The head wound didn't seem to be more than a lump, but who could tell? She had heard of concussion cases that simply slipped deeper and deeper into unconsciousness until death came.

Sara and Hanno were eating a meal of sorts. Only two days before, Sara would not have called it a meal at all, and they were eating it out of their hands, standing up on a pitching deck. Bread, green olives, a chunk of smoked meat, a piece of cheese, and a shared cup of watered wine.

"So if the wind's blowing from the east, we're going west," said Sara, looking up at the sail.

"Yes. Just as well, too. We're out of the gulf now, and there's nothing but sea between us and the Pillars. There's nowhere else to go, anyway. Palestine, if we could reach it. Only we can't. The wind is against."

Sara nodded. "I told them that we were bound for the Fortunate Isles," she said, staring down at the ship's wake. "It was the farthest place I could think of."

Her father moved uneasily beside her. He also was standing on the weather side of the upper deck, his hands on the rail. The weather side was the proper side to be on, since the lee side was needed for the steersman and the lee-side rudder. Sara had recently learned the difference between lee and weather, and between port and starboard, which were not the same. She was becoming less surprised now at how important such things were aboard ship.

"Yes, I heard," said Hanno. He sounded a little impatient. "That was the right thing to say, but I should have been the one who made the decision. The Romans will not follow us out into the Ocean Sea and won't follow at all if they hear that we have gone there. Gaul and Britain are too far north for the season, so it has to be the Fortunate Isles—but it should have been me who told them."

Sara nodded, abstracted. She was trying to understand the sharp little needle of resentment that she felt when he said that their heading should have been his decision. Of course it should have been Father who made the decision. It was his ship, wasn't it? And he was Father, wasn't he? It wasn't her place to give orders. It was his.

But he hadn't been capable of it at the time. It had been up to her.

Hanno straightened. He folded his arms, turned, and leaned against the stern rail. "But it doesn't matter anyway. You told them the right thing. It might look a little...But it doesn't matter."

Doesn't matter? Suddenly, Sara couldn't keep silent. She found herself shaking with anger, though she didn't know exactly why. "Doesn't matter? You think it doesn't matter that I had to do it all?" She rounded on him fiercely, astonished at her own sudden fury. He was clearly astonished by it, too, staring at her, his mouth dropping open. For some reason that only enraged her more. She gestured furiously. "*Sensible* Sara, *calm* Sara, *reliable* Sara! I did this. I'm the one who tore us away from our lives. We could have died, like Aram. And *now* you approve. Oh, how very generous of you! And you say it doesn't matter. Well, it *does* matter, and your approval has come too late. It's done now, and *I* did it. But do you think I wanted to be the one it all depends on?" She was shouting now. She felt her hands balling into fists at her side, the rage possessing her like a demon. *"Why did you leave me to do it all?"*

It might have been almost comical, the way he goggled. Then he seemed to swell. His face became thunderous. "How dare you? How *dare* you? You do *not* have the right to speak to me that way, Sara. I am your father...."

"Then act like one! Fathers protect. Fathers *do* things. Fathers make it..." Rage choked her.

"Make it what? Make it all go away?" He was shouting, too, looming over her. She thought for a moment that he would strike her. "Do you think I don't want it all to go away? Do you think that I don't want it to be over? I can't make it go away!"

"You..." She didn't really know what she was about to say. Something about Aram. Something meant to hurt, something dreadful, something unforgivable. But she could not go on. "You made me do..."

"I made you do nothing. Nothing! You did it all yourself. And why?" His voice broke. He wheeled and stared out at the heaving sea, then turned back. The question had silenced her, and he saw it and followed up. "Why did you do it? You've said it yourself. We could have died." His face crumpled, and his head bowed. "Like Aram, like Aram, my son, my son. We should be dead, like him." He was rocking backward and forward, weeping, striking at his chest.

Sara shook her head in furious rejection. "No. No. I didn't mean..." And she hadn't. There was nothing right about dying. "I never said we should die. Don't you dare accuse me of it!" And then, in a raw scream: "Do you think Aram would want that?"

Aram, tall, laughing Aram. She closed her eyes and saw his face, and for a time there was only the pain.

It receded slowly and again became background. The world forced itself on her again. Silence, but for the sounds of the sea. She opened her eyes.

Hanno was staring at her. His hands were at the neck of his tunic, about to rend it. Some demon seized control of her tongue. Or perhaps it was the real Sara, the sharp one who lived inside her head: "And don't tear your garment. I'll only have to mend it. It's not as though you have plenty of others now."

For a moment, she thought he would bridle again. His eyes closed and his face tightened, the jutting beak of his nose becoming a blade. He had lost weight already, she saw, some cold, distant part of her mind noting it, just as it noted the swell of the sea and the creaking of the rigging and the slow roll of the ship. Then his eyes opened again, and they locked on her. His hands dropped to his side. Father and daughter seemed to stare at each other for a long time.

"You always were the practical one," he whispered at last. Then he shook his head and sighed. "My dear, my dear. I'm so sorry.... It wasn't good enough. I didn't mean to slight you."

He took a deep breath. "You're right. You shouldn't have had to do it all. It was my task, and I failed in it. I failed you. I'm sorry, and I'll try to do better."

It only turned her remaining rage into tears. Her hands came up to cover her face. He stepped forward, and she felt his tentative touch. She stood rigid for a moment, then laid her head on his shoulder and wept.

"What's to become of us?" she asked, when she could form words. "We have nothing anymore, we *are* nothing anymore."

He took time to answer. "We have a ship. We have a cargo. We have ourselves. We have each other. I've had much less than that in my time. I'm still a trader, and I am *not* going to throw away what you have done. Aram would never approve, as you say. We go on. That's all. We go on. We do whatever we have to do. We survive."

It sounded to Sara as if he were trying to convince himself. They stood there together.

He breathed in, and it was clear that he was forcing his mind to practical matters. "We'll need water and provisions soon. And ship's stores. Rope. Sailcloth. Spare spars if we can get them. We'll have to look in at Tarbarca." That was the small port west of Carthage, a full day's sail along the coast. House Harcar sometimes ran cargoes into there, if the Romans were blockading the city.

He pointed with his chin at the distant shore to port, a blue line on the edge of the world. "That's Cape Soan, there. The wind is fair for Tarbarca. We'll be there by dusk at this rate. Aratian will have heard already, most like, though we've come pretty fast. Always first with the news, Aratian."

She nodded but let it pass, then turned her head to stare at the distant coast. It didn't matter. Father would take charge of it now. She could let go, just a little.

She had been across to Tarbarca once by land, an uncomfortable two-day journey in a horse-litter. Father and Aram had escorted her on a visit to distant cousins who, in turn, had connections with a noble family that happened to have two unmarried sons. It had only occurred to Sara later that she was being shown off. Both the sons were graceless oafs, one a mouth breather, the other with a tendency to giggle, and neither had displayed the slightest evidence of intelligence. Sara had been bored rigid. Of course that would have been of little importance, if Father had decided that a match was desirable, but nothing was ever said. Sara suspected that Aram had talked Father out of it.

It was like tearing the scab off a wound, Sara thought. Something would remind her, and the tears began again, as painful as ever. She had to distract herself. With an effort she recalled Aratian, Hanno's agent in Tarbarca. He was a Greek.

The harbor at Tarbarca was no more than an inlet with a single pier, and the news of a ship arriving got around the small town as soon as the sail could be seen coming in. Aratian was among a group on the pier when they came into the little port late in the afternoon, and he boarded immediately, a narrow-eyed, balding man in a linen tunic. Naturally, everyone wanted news, and *Heron* was wearing the Harcar house pennant. He marched straight up to the afterdeck, the only slightly private place in the ship, not waiting for an invitation.

Sara was present, of course. The alternative was to leave her unchaperoned among the rough sailors. She pretended to be mending clothes, seated on a stool, and oblivious. They spoke Greek, which might have made the conversation more private. Not much, though. Sara, for example, could speak it, and certainly the captain had made voyages there. It was the trade language, after all.

"So it's true," Aratian said with no preamble, as soon as he arrived on the afterdeck.

Hanno, of course, was giving nothing away. Always a sound principle. "Depends," he replied. "What have you heard?"

Aratian made an impatient gesture. "That the Romans won a great battle in the south, at a place called Zama, and they destroyed the whole army. They're in full march for the city, and there's no stopping them. They're probably there now, in fact."

"And that's all you know?"

"Isn't that enough?"

Hanno ignored the question. "The city can stand a long siege. The walls are strong."

"If that's so, why are you here and not there?"

"Why should I take chances? Anyway, a city under siege is no place to conduct business. Most likely the Senate has already confiscated all the food stocks and forbidden most trade."

"That's if there're any senators who haven't fled."

Hanno's head jerked up at that, staring straight into the Greek's face. He said nothing for a moment. Then: "I am on a trading venture, sailing west—to Spain, maybe the Fortunate Isles—carrying spices, olive oil, wine, dates, linen. I'll be needing to reprovision. My captain has a list..."

"How will you pay?"

Hanno's brows drew down. "As a trading credit against the debt you owe me, of course."

"What debt? I owe you nothing." The words came out flat, as if certain, but Sara, abandoning any pretense of mending, was looking into the sly little eyes as it was said, and she saw the gloating there.

"You received four cargoes last month on my behalf. I have the ladings...." said Hanno, clearly unable to credit his ears, thinking still that this must be some honest mistake. Sara knew different. No. This was not a mistake.

"Those? I had to sell for a loss. There's no market, what with the Romans blocking the port. People are hoarding their money."

The senator's face suddenly cleared. "Ah," he said. Pause. "A loss, you say. How much of a loss?"

Aratian pursed his lips. He seemed a little taken aback, as if he had expected anger. "Why...it would amount to four thousand drachmas or so. Twenty Carthaginian pounds of silver."

"Alas, indeed." Hanno groaned. Yet his face seemed almost cheerful. He shook his head, and in the gesture Sara could see a sort of mockery. "A dreadful loss. Why, that amounts to more than I actually paid for the cargoes. To lose that much, you must have *paid* people to take the goods away. You'd have done better if you'd dropped them straight into the harbor."

The Greek flushed and bit his lip. "That's the total. There were other losses in the last year. This war..."

"Yes. Quite. It has had terrible effects on trade." Hanno

paced to the forward rail, staring down the length of the deck. He nodded. "All confidence and trust is gone. And all honesty, too." He turned. "By an interesting coincidence, this ship and cargo would be worth about twenty pounds of silver on the old market. No doubt you have mentioned this fact to your friends. But of course, by your account, the goods are worth nothing whatsoever, as things stand now. Less than nothing. In fact, it seems I would be doing you a favor by taking anything in your warehouse off your hands at no cost to you. Shall we go and inspect?"

The Greek said nothing. A faint shake of the head, as if the question were not worth the breath required to speak it, then he turned away and walked the two steps down to the main deck. Hanno smiled, then lifted his hand. Two men had come to the gangway when Hanno had moved to the forward rail. One of them, Sara saw, was the captain, and the other the little castaway, Jerem. They turned. There was a sudden, subtle movement. Aratian stopped short.

"Bring him back," said Hanno wearily.

The captain and Jerem sauntered up, one on each side of the Greek. Aratian glanced down at Jerem's face, which wore a gentle smile, then at the small man's nearer hand. He turned and mounted the step again without a word.

Sara couldn't see what was in Jerem's hand. Nor in the captain's either.

The Greek's face was shiny with sweat and stiff with fear. "You can't..." he began.

Jerem smiled a little wider and appeared to nudge him in a good-humored way. "Shut up," he said affably. Aratian jerked and paled noticeably.

"His seal?" asked Hanno.

The captain shook his head in a sorrowful fashion. "Between his tunic and his belt. I can see it from here."

"Bring him." Hanno had produced a wax stick and a paper. He held the stick in the flame of the stern lantern for a moment. Sara had wondered why it was lit in broad daylight.

The wax was dripped on the paper. Hanno presented it, and Aratian was nudged again. Again his eyes went to Jerem's hand. Jerem smiled gently again, and Aratian groped in his tunic and brought out a carved stone seal. He sealed the paper, moving stiffly, like one who has a pain in his side.

"All right," said Hanno. He handed the paper to the captain. "You'll need three men. I'll entertain my former agent and colleague in the cabin. I feel sure that our new steward, here, will be all the servants we'll need. Get whatever you can, but take no more than half an hour."

The captain nodded. He took the paper, turned, and walked down to the deck. A single word, and three men followed him across the gangplank and down the dock.

"Shall we?" asked Hanno, smiling, with a courteous gesture. He led the way into the cabin. Aratian followed, walking stiffly, little Jerem solicitously at his elbow in case he should stumble on the step. Sara picked up her mending and her stool and followed them, head downcast, in the proper and dutiful posture. She wasn't going to miss this.

The stern cabin was as it had been. There was barely room for all of them. One cot was folded, and the hammock was stowed away. The other cot still held the Roman. He appeared to be still asleep, or maybe dying. Or maybe not.

Sara noted automatically that there was no discharge on the bandage, and that he was pale, not fevered.

Hanno crouched under the deck beams. He was taller than the rest of them. "Sit," he said, pointing at the stern locker. He dropped the cot and sat on it. Jerem kindly assisted Aratian to a seat, then stood politely beside him, as if ready to pour wine. Sara put her stool down and sat, her knees almost touching her father's.

"Now we wait," said Hanno. "But not for long."

Aratian's eyes darted, white in the gloom. "You'll never—"

"Get away with this?" Hanno smiled. "Do you know, I rather think we will. Who are you going to complain to? The Romans?"

"I have only to shout."

"Ah. But you won't shout, dear old friend and colleague, because that would cause you to get rather a bad pain in the throat. Not that shouting would summon your friends on the dock, not now. I recognized three of them myself before we tied up, and no doubt Captain Obala knows others. Aratian, you never did understand that you have to pay what things actually cost. I bet you've paid the minimum. Do you really think that people like Big Taglus and Loukie One-Eye will stay hired by you if I offer them half an obol more?"

Sara was staring at Hanno Harcar's shadowed face as if she were seeing it for the first time. In a sense, she was. The Senator of the City had disappeared, and her beloved father had been transformed. He had said he would not fail her again.

"An important lesson in commercial ethics, my dear," said Hanno, and Sara, absorbed in her own thoughts, realized with a shock that he was talking to her. She looked up, startled. "Rule one: Play by the rules, where they apply. Rule two: If they don't apply, then don't play by them. This idiot"—he indicated Aratian—"thought that he could throw away just some of them, and the rest would still be respected."

"Bad business sense," said Jerem. "He should know better, him being in the shipping trade and all."

Father nodded in agreement. "Tcha! Greeks! They're either too civilized or not civilized enough. I'm so glad we had that conversation, my boy. You're quite right. Everyone's a weasel. You'll go far in the shipping business yourself, I think."

Aratian opened his mouth to speak. Hanno just shook his head, and a steel gleam appeared under Aratian's chin. The Greek stiffened into rigidity, his eyes showing terrified white in the gloom. Sara hadn't seen Jerem's hands move.

"Shut up," said Hanno, his voice echoing.

They waited, wordless. The captain's return was announced by a volley of orders and a creaking of ropes. Sara resisted the urge to turn and look through the curtain to see what they were doing on the main deck. She listened instead.

Something thumped down, and the ship lurched a little. "Lash it down, there. Now the cordage. Lower away."

A few minutes later, the captain himself parted the curtain. "Stores aboard, sir. They even had a spare mainyard and plenty of sailcloth. We can get water up the coast a way. I know a place."

"Very good. How's the wind?"

"It'll serve."

"Then let us go."

The captain swung around, dropping the curtain. Sara

listened to the footfalls and the shouts. She was watching her father. His expression had changed again. He was staring at the sweating Greek agent with a face of stone.

"What are you going to do with him?" she asked, but it was Jerem who answered.

"Miss," he said, "I think you might want to go up on deck." He was watching Hanno, waiting.

Aratian moaned through rigid lips. Crimson and stark white chased each other across his bald head. Sara shuddered. Hanno's eyes turned slowly to her face, and with a cold shock she saw something there she had never thought possible. She felt herself blanch.

He continued to regard her, his face remote. "I think Jerem might be right," he said slowly. "I'm not giving him a chance to improve his offer to his employees on the dock, and we certainly can't manage another prisoner. You should go out on deck."

She shook her head, not taking her eyes off him. For an unmeasured time she could not speak. Then: "No. Please, no. Father, there are . . . there are some rules that cannot be broken, no matter what other people do."

Again he said nothing but looked back at Jerem. For a long, hanging moment his face showed no change at all. Aratian saw that face, and he whimpered again. Abruptly, his bladder released. Nobody moved.

Then Hanno breathed out. He shook his head at Jerem. "No," he said. "We'll get rid of him another way."

CHAPTER 6

They dropped the Greek into the sea fifty paces off the point, at a place where the current set in. With him went a cork float to support him as he swam for shore.

"If it was up to me, it'd be a rock, tied around his neck," growled Obala, watching from the deck.

"That was my first thought, too," said Hanno. "Certainly he won't thank us for his life. And he'll make himself handy to the Romans, no doubt. Make much of his Greek citizenship. But I can't kill people just because I think they deserve it, and certainly not in front of my daughter. Perhaps I've lost my edge. Jerem might think so." Hanno pursed his lips as his former agent kicked in the water. "Aratian's an islander, Naxian or Parian, I believe. They can all swim."

"A Cretan, more like. I can't tell the accent, but those bastards can lie in every language in the world."

A pause while Hanno looked up at the sail. "Weather's still holding," he remarked after a moment.

"Aye, maybe. If the wind comes round west, we might be in for a blow...."

Their voices faded. Sara heard the footsteps as they crossed the deck above. She bent again to her mending. The light was dim in the cabin, but she had to watch her patient.

"Not a good idea."

Sara looked up. The voice was unfamiliar—rusty, croaking, but with a ludicrously cultured accent, the Greek sounding stately and sonorous. She turned her head.

It was the Roman, of course. His eyes were open. He was craning his neck to see through the narrow gap in the curtain, and the effort made him wince, but he still kept doing it.

"Lie back," said Sara crossly. And then: "What isn't a good idea?"

"You telling your father to let that Greek go, of course. Slimy little sod, trying it on like that. *My* father would have strung him up."

Sara's brows rose. "Be thankful my father doesn't string people up, then. You'd be a candidate."

Once, she would have been sure about that, about Hanno not killing. With a shock, she realized she wasn't sure anymore that it was true. "So you've been awake for hours," she added. She was rewarded by a look of wide-eyed innocence. Green eyes, she saw. "Oh, please. You've been listening to everything we say—that's obvious. But why wake up now?"

A smile, although his lips were chapped and cracking. "Ah. Well, it might have been because I saw the chance to talk to you alone." The smile became gallant, with a touch of practiced wistfulness. Sara snorted. The Roman made a modest gesture. "But mostly it's because I need...ah...a pot."

Without words, Sara turned and put her head through the curtain. The small man was sitting on the step to the quarterdeck, cleaning his nails with his knife. "Jerem," she asked, making her tone polite. He looked up. "Would you be so good as to find a necessary pot for our guest?" She remembered the Roman's cracked lips and his croaking voice. "And some water. In a different vessel. And then tie him up again. I see he's been working on his bonds." Jerem nodded and slipped below.

She waited until he returned, his hands full. Then she rose without haste and left, pulling the curtain decisively shut behind her. From the main deck the day was bright, the breeze cool on her cheek. Hanno was standing on the upper deck, and she climbed the steep little steps to stand beside him at the rail.

"I didn't know the Romans spoke Greek," she remarked after a moment. Something about the fellow irritated her, apart from the fact that he was a Roman. She couldn't think what it was.

Her father looked down at her, one eyebrow quirking. "They don't, usually," he said. "They speak their own language, one that nobody else speaks."

"This one speaks Greek. But he doesn't speak it as we do, or like that fellow who tried to cheat you." A steady wind was pushing *Heron* westward, with the African coast just in sight to port. "He speaks it as though he's got a pebble in his mouth, all rounded and hollow."

Hanno nodded. "Ah, well, now. That's one more proof that he's one of their nobles. They call themselves a republic, you know, but Rome is really ruled by a small group of aristocratic families. This young man will be from one of them. He's learned to speak Attic Greek, gone to Athens and Thebes on tour, and been tutored by a Greek philosopher. They do that with their sons, if they're rich enough."

"Why?" Sara was genuinely puzzled. Greeks were scattered all over the known world, having fled their own country. That was because it was poor and stony, and the Greeks themselves were quarrelsome, treacherous, and violent. They were found everywhere, so their language was handy, but nobody thought anything good about them.

The senator shrugged. "Yes, I know it sounds odd, but the Roman upper class admires the Greeks. They think Greeks are civilized and sophisticated. Well, so they are, compared to Romans." He sighed. "I used to have a little sideline running Parian marble and Attic pottery into Rome, through an agent. That's gone now, of course. It was worthwhile for a time, though."

Sara realized, with a shock, that her father was discussing politics and business with her.

"I thought Rome was closed to all trade with Carthage," she said, covering her surprise.

"Officially. But wherever there are sellers and buyers, there is always trade, and Romans are rather good at looking the other way if it suits them. The agent I had was a client of one of the big houses. The aristocrats want to be thought genteel, though their taste runs to the gaudy, like all barbarians. They buy luxury goods—spices, gems, silks, art. That sort of thing. That's apart from the Egyptian grain trade, but the Rhodeans have got that sewn up."

Sara felt as one must feel on being initiated into the Mysteries. Her father was addressing her as an adult. Almost as he had spoken to Aram, this year or so, before... Sara snatched her mind away from that thought like a hand from a hot stove.

She covered it with another question: "What have we to trade now, though?"

Hanno grimaced. "Well. *Heron* was just in from an eastern voyage, and she hasn't been unloaded. We've got wine from Palestine, sweeter than they have in the west. Greek olive oil, and Colombaean olives, better than the local. Linen from Egypt, which will sell well in Spain, if we can run in there. And maybe half a ton of Cypriot almonds and pistachios. Not so good, that. The only real market is Carthage itself, or Rome. Then there's your spices, and we also have coin."

"And what would we want for them?"

"Metals, mainly, in the west. Always buy at the source, if you can. Silver and tin in ingots. Spanish steel. Even gold. Carded wool, maybe, but it would have to be fine. Maybe dyes—madder and indigo, even murex. Purple, that is. It depends."

"On what's available?"

"On price. But there's something else that almost works for us. See, the navy used to keep pirates down. But there is no navy of Carthage anymore. So the pirates are flourishing."

Sara stared at him, struggling to understand. "How can that work for us?"

"It eliminates competition in the carrying trade. Sellers will have goods on their hands. Buyers elsewhere are starved for them. We can buy for less and sell for more. *Heron* is fast and handy, much better than most. I had her built to run goods into Carthage in the teeth of the Roman blockade, after all. She should be able to outrun any pirate, if there's a decent wind."

His face showed nothing but shrewd calculation, a balancing of odds. Sara, appalled, looked past him at the shimmering water, and it came to her suddenly that her whole world had been turned into sea, treacherous, full of shifting currents and sudden storms, offering no place to stand. How strange! The world had always felt so firm and secure, before. Had it really been founded on thousands of calculations like these?

"But that's why I think we needn't go outside the Gates. The straits swarm with corsairs, and anyway the Fortunate Islands are small and poor. It's fine to have the Romans think we've gone there, but I think we should try for Spain or Gaul."

The captain stumped up from the main deck. He nodded at a distant point of land off to port, a salient of Africa. "Cape Harka," he said, as though the name should mean something. "If we want to make Narbon in Gaul, we should turn north now."

Hanno pulled at his beard. "Hmm. Lepida in Spain would be better. There's the silver mines there, and enough local moneyed gentry that want our wine and so on. Buy at source, sell at distance, that's my motto."

"Big risk. Last time I was there, the Romans didn't have a garrison, but there could be one by now. If there is, the local magistrate won't be able to look the other way, even though he might want to."

"Well, maybe. Only one way to find out." Hanno ruminated. "How's your Greek?"

"Fair, but I'll never pass for one, if that's what you're thinking."

"Hmm. Well, I can manage." Hanno was looking at Sara thoughtfully. She stared back. "And I think you can, too." Then he nodded sharply. "Lepida," he said.

Heron swung about, heading north, leaving Africa behind. Sara turned to watch the crew bracing the yard around, the steersman leaning against the tiller. She didn't realize at first that her father was speaking to her again.

"How's your patient?"

"Mending. Now that he's awake, I think we must walk him about on deck."

"Is that wise?"

"Perhaps not, but if he doesn't stretch that leg, the scar will contract, and he'll always favor it."

"He'll have to be watched, then. Jerem says he works at his bonds all the time nobody's around. A determined young man. Typically Roman. He's probably got some notion of breaking free, diving over the side, and swimming to shore."

Sara was watching Africa recede into the gathering haze. Dusk was coming. The new course was taking the ship steadily out to sea. "That would be foolish now."

"It would be foolish at any time. But he's a Roman. Their language has fourteen different words for 'stubborn,' none of them adequate."

She looked up at her father. "You sound almost as if you admired them."

His face creased, and he swept a glance over the ship. "In

a way, I do. They're endlessly resilient, able to absorb terrible blows and still keep going. In Italy, Hannibal destroyed their whole army not just once, but twice over, but they never dreamed of coming to terms. They just kept on fighting, and eventually they wore him down with small raids, ambushes, and cutting off his supplies. When he left Italy he was still undefeated in the field, but the Romans had won anyway."

"You never told me that before. Just that he'd destroyed every army sent against him."

"Mmm. And that was the truth. But here's a strange thing. The best lies are entirely true, in themselves. A truth is *all* the truth."

Sara nodded, folded her arms, and stared forward, past the ship's bow and into the marching blue unknown. "So," she said carefully, after a moment. "You were telling me a lie, then."

Only a few days ago, she would never have said such a thing to him. Now she found herself watching his face, trying to guess at his thoughts.

He glanced down at her, then went on studying the set of the sail and the pattern the rigging made against the lightened sky. The planes of his face seemed harder than before, and she remembered the look in his eyes as he had considered Aratian's fate. She had been watching a stranger.

"Is it a lie if you believe it yourself?" he asked after a moment. Sara said nothing. She knew he was asking the question of himself. "Did I actually believe it?" He shook his head. "Certainly I wanted to. And I did believe that we would survive. I believed that Hannibal had won and would win again. And so I sent Aram. Yet in another way I knew that Hannibal had lost, and I knew he might lose again. And still I sent Aram."

Sara realized, with a shock, that he was weeping. She had never seen that, never. Not even at Mother's pyre. Not even then. Yet his face was now as it was then, a mask carved as though from wood. Only the tears moved on it.

"No," she said, turning toward him. "That wasn't how it happened. I remember. He wanted to go and pestered you about it for months. And still you wouldn't allow him, until you heard that the Carbata had sent their two sons. If the richest family in the city had done as much, how could we do less?"

Hanno's eyes closed, but his face remained unchanged, and his voice was steady. "And how is that better? No matter how much I wanted to believe otherwise, I knew in my heart that I was sending him to his death. And in the end, I did it anyway, because my pride required that I match the Carbata." His expression changed then, becoming the face of a judge who pronounces sentence. "I failed him, and I failed you. But I shall not fail again."

Sara looked into his face again. Again, it might have been the face of a stranger.

CHAPTER 7

Don't like it," muttered Obala ten days later, approaching the dock at Lepida. A slow passage had made him fretful. "That tub's a Roman. Has to be. Nobody else builds 'em so clumsy. That's just a packing crate with a mast." He was speaking without moving his lips, as though the large ship berthed at the deeper of Lepida's two docks wasn't half a mile away across the placid water.

"At least she's not a warship," said Hanno. He, too, was staring at it.

"She'll have Roman soldiers aboard, though. They always do. That makes it hard to tell the difference sometimes."

"Yes, but at least there won't be a government official. They wouldn't be traveling like that. Too slow. Whoever this is will just be trading for steel blanks or iron pigs or maybe silver." Hanno inspected the ship again. "Most likely he won't bother his head about us, but if he does, we can easily outrun him."

Obala nodded toward the docks. "There's the harbormaster's boat now."

"I'll handle him. Keep the crew quiet."

The harbormaster, a native Hispanian, didn't bother to board. The conversation was conducted in hails across the still water. Hanno identified himself as Cleontes, son of Lartes, a Rhodean, in wine and eastern goods, trading for silver, or maybe tin.

"You'll be needing a berth, then. Lucky we're not busy," said the harbormaster.

"Not I. It's not worth the demurrage fees, and I don't want to be stuck here windbound if there's a shift. We'll anchor in the offing and load from lighters."

"Suit yourself. Costs about the same to hire the lighters. Slower, too, of course."

"Maybe. I won't be shifting much tonnage. *Heron*'s no pig-iron carrier, like that tub yonder. Is there a shore boat?"

"My cousin will take you in. I'll tell him on the way back. Anchor inside the point there, out of the fairway."

"Certainly." Hanno watched the boat pull away. "Well, that was free and easy. He wouldn't have been so casual about it if there'd been a Roman official here."

Obala grunted. "Not busy," he says. Have a look at that second berth. Those rub marks are a year old if they're a day. Been that long since they've had two ships in at once." He shook his head. "The Romans will have to do something about the piracy problem. It's strangling trade."

"One man's problem is another man's opportunity."

"Huh." The captain raised his voice. "Shorten sail. Haul it up. Stand by to let go the anchor."

A boat was already on its way out to meet them. Hanno watched its approach. Others were drawn up on the beach, idle. "The fishing can't be much good, either. Or they're frightened to go out. I wonder how much this one has paid to become the harbormaster's cousin."

Sara shook her head. She went below while Hanno haggled for the fare. Those stitches in the Roman's leg needed to come out now that the wound was joined and they were anchored in a quiet harbor.

"He says he hasn't had his walk today, miss," said Jerem sometime later. Dusk was coming on.

Sara hissed between her teeth. No, the Roman had not been walked that day. The winds had been contrary and shifty, the crew had been busy, and she had forgotten. Still she shook her head. "Well, he's not going on deck, not now. He can wait until we're at sea again. He understands most of what we say, I'm sure. He might know that there's Roman-held land not more than a long swim away, and I believe he'd be fool enough to think he can reach it."

Jerem looked sour, sucking his teeth. "Miss, that's for sure, and he might even be right at that. He's exercising that leg every minute he gets, and it looks fine, but he's still limping. I think he's foxing us."

They were talking in Punic, the Carthaginian language, standing in the hold, crouched under the main deck beams. Sara had just finished removing the Roman soldier's stitches, and the pink wound was drained and healing. No need for a bandage now. The patient hadn't made a sound when she pulled the threads out. He had only stared gravely at the planking overhead as though it contained secrets he wished to puzzle out.

"What are you saying?" he asked now, from his hammock, cheerfully, as if joining in a friendly conversation.

"Not to trust you for a moment." Sara spoke in Greek, not bothering to raise her voice. She switched back to Punic. "All right, Jerem. Get him his dinner. I'll watch him. He can't get to me before I call for help, and you won't be more than twenty feet away."

"He touches you, miss, I'll hang him, living, with his own skin for a rope." Jerem bestowed a last glare on the Roman, then went forward to where the supplies were stored, moving out of sight around the lashed-down cargo.

The Roman held up his bound hands. "I'm hardly going to bite through the cords you just retied so tightly and leap on you." He stared at the bonds. "Actually, I think they're too tight. My fingers are turning blue," he added hopefully.

Sara glanced sidelong. "Very pretty. The color suits you."

He looked hurt. "If you were my guest..."

"I'm not. You're not *my* guest, either. You're Father's. Think yourself lucky you're not feeding the fish."

"Well, possibly that might cost you a ransom. Possibly. Mind you, I can't say for sure that my own father would actually pay one. Quite likely not, I think."

The words were calm, matter-of-fact. Sara found herself staring at him. He seemed quite serious. "Would your father rather see you sold than pay a ransom?" she asked. "Or simply have your throat cut?"

He nodded, quite seriously. "Possibly. I'm only the third son," he said, as if that explained everything. Then with a look of pure chagrin: "Oh, whatever am I thinking? Where are my manners? My tutor said that aboard ship, it is acceptable to introduce oneself rather than wait to be introduced. So then: I am Marcus Licinius Corbo. My father is the senator, once consul, Quintus Licinius Corbo. As you can see by that, his was a truly Roman upbringing."

Sara shook her head. "How can I see that?" she asked.

"Why, from his name. Quintus. It just means 'the fifth.' In his family, sons were given numbers." Marcus frowned. "I think it was my mother who made sure I was given an actual name. In his heart of hearts, Father probably still thinks it's a little soft and decadent to do that. Hence my doubts about his paying a ransom, you see. He's a real Roman." It was said with a strange, wry pride.

"Numbers? You Romans give your children numbers, not names?"

A tiny shrug. "Why not? It makes perfect sense, in a way."

"So does breathing water, but only if you're a fish."

He blinked, and his green eyes opened wide. "You know, I never really thought of it that way," he said.

Sara studied the innocence on his face for a moment. Then: "No, of course not. It never crossed your mind for an instant. Not now, not when you toured Greece, not ever. The thought has never occurred to you that other peoples have different ways, and if their ways are strange to you, that yours will be strange to them." She snorted. "And I am Dido, queen of Carthage. How do you do?"

He grinned openly. "Well, my name really is Marcus, Your Highness."

Sara folded her arms and leaned back against a hull frame. After a moment: "Sara bih-Hanno is mine. Sara, daughter of Hanno."

"Ah. Master Hanno, the merchant who dropped that

Greek thief overboard. Don't be surprised if you come to regret that."

"Dropping him overboard?"

"Letting him live."

"As I remarked before, we let *you* live." And then: "But I agree with you, incidentally. Letting you live is bad practice, too." He simply smiled, and she realized with chagrin that he knew it had been said for effect and was untrue.

"Yes, no doubt." He stretched. "I'm *so* glad we're both in the minority on that question."

At that, Jerem returned with a wooden bowl of cold bean porridge with bacon and a piece of cheese. Marcus inclined his head regally and held his hands out to be untied. There was the merest flicker of movement, too fast to follow, and a hard thud. A knife was quivering, its point buried two fingers deep in the tough wood next to the head of the hammock, about a hand span from Marcus's left eye. "You can reach that, if you try," said Jerem pleasantly. "Go ahead and try. I've got others."

Sara wet her lips. She hadn't seen Jerem's hand move. "He says..." she began.

"I believe I understand," said Marcus. He lowered his bound hands, moving very carefully. "He has a way of making himself clear." He waited while he was loosed, took the bowl, and began to eat, keeping both hands in sight. Jerem folded his arms and watched him.

"So," asked Marcus, between bites, "where are we?"

Sara considered her answer. "At anchor."

"Well, I know that. I heard the anchor cable rattling out."

He looked closely at Sara, but she said nothing. The less Marcus knew, the better. If he knew that there was a Roman ship a few hundred paces away, he might do something silly. "Let me see how close I can get, then. Last time you let me up on deck we were out of sight of land, and the sun was too high to use it to find direction, but still I had the notion that we were headed west and north. It's been ten days, but I've heard a lot of hauling in the middle of the night, which means unreliable winds. So...it's Corsica, maybe, or Gaul, or it could be nearer to Spain. Or the Balearic Islands. Hum. Pretty wide choice." He had glanced at her face with each of his suggestions, but Sara was her father's daughter. Her face had apparently told him nothing.

"You forgot Mauretania, or Nubia beyond the Pillars of Herakles, or the Fortunate Isles," she replied, deadpan.

"No, no." Marcus waggled a playful finger. "You couldn't have gone that far, and if you had, you need never have been out of sight of land."

"If you say so. Though if you're basing your estimate on the sailing rate of one of your Roman tubs, think again. And Carthaginians sail the blue water, not hug the coast. We are kings of the sea."

Marcus looked up. He was staring her straight in the eyes. "You *were*. Past tense." The roguish note had gone from his voice. She raised an eyebrow but said nothing. "So, now," he asked, "how are you going to convey this ransom demand? Assuming my father would pay."

"I imagine *my* father will find a way. There are go-betweens, I understand."

"Oh, quite so. I was present—let me see, it was eight

months ago—at the execution of several of them. In Sicily, that was. But the war may be over now. Either that, or Carthage really has been destroyed, which amounts to the same thing. Perhaps the Senate will tolerate trade again. Who knows?" He chewed reflectively. "One thing's for sure, though. They'll insist on the immediate return of prisoners, without ransom, and they won't differentiate between state prisoners and those in private hands. Anyone who ignores that will be treated simply as a pirate."

He had finally unsettled her. She bridled, with a sharp breath.

"What's he saying, miss?" asked Jerem, his hand going to his side. "Maybe he needs to be learned some manners." Jerem clearly knew no Greek.

"No. It's all right. He's just being silly." She switched back to Greek. "Being treated as a pirate by Rome doesn't seem to amount to much, apart from being ignored. We can stand that, I think."

He didn't bother to deny it but nevertheless shook his head. "Rome has been distracted. That will change, no doubt."

"I'll let you know if it does. Have you finished?"

"Thank you. I have."

"Jerem, if you'd be so good. And make sure he's secure." She cocked her head. That was the boat returning. She climbed the ladder to the deck.

Hanno came aboard, blandly smiling. That changed once the boat had pulled away again. His face went blank. "Sara, I'll need you tomorrow. For your Greek."

"Trouble?" asked Obala.

"Not exactly. But we'll have to be convincing. There's news.

A fast galley passed three days ago with it. The war in Africa is over. It's peace." He turned and regarded Sara. Her rush of relief and joy was fleeting. It wouldn't bring Aram back, and there was something in Hanno's face. His next words confirmed it. "The Romans didn't even sack the city—in return for a small payment. Ten thousand talents of silver, or the same in gold. A big ship, loaded to the rail with bullion."

"What? How much...?" Obala gaped. "Ten thousand... great gods, there isn't that much money in the world!"

Sara was staring, too. For a time, she could only gasp. But then: "Ten thousand talents? That's more than the output of the Spanish mines in ten years. More than..." She was calculating, despite herself. "But that will create enormous demand for silver. And gold, too. Carthage will have to beggar itself to obtain so much. The price will..." And then the reaction took her. Aram was dead, and for what? A weight of precious metal? If Carthage had paid rather than fight the battle, wouldn't he still be alive?

But Hanno was nodding. "The price of metals will shoot up. Anywhere outside Rome. Exactly. And the silver miners here know it, but they don't realize by how much. They're thinking half as much again. But I know how much the city had, and how much it'll have to find, and I'm thinking triple. But if I run it into Carthage, they'll need it a bit too much, and there's little to trade for it. I'm buying silver, therefore, but I'm taking it to Alexandria."

"They're willing to sell here?"

"Oh, yes." Hanno sounded a little distracted. "I spent all of today establishing my good name and finding out what they'd consider a fair price. A fair price, because that Roman purser is a fool. He's offering rock bottom and leaning on the locals to accept, with vague threats of Roman displeasure if they don't. Might as well be a pirate himself." Hanno simply shook his head, but Sara almost gasped. There was that word again. "He doesn't like competition, either. He was following me around, to see how much I was offering. I think he thought I didn't notice. Well, I did. We'll see tomorrow."

CHAPTER 8

Sodding Romans. Lousy cheap grubs. D'ye know what that weasel-faced little toe-rag was offering me for these? And telling me that I'd better not sell to anyone he doesn't approve of?"

The swordsmith laid one of a sheaf of sword blades on his counter. Hanno picked it up and examined it, nodding a little to himself. It hadn't been honed or polished yet, and no crossguard, grip, or pommel had been fitted, but, held slantwise to the light, even Sara could see the patterns of swirling steel in the surface.

"Fine work," murmured Hanno. "Mind you, you wouldn't expect to get last year's price, the war being over and all."

The smith snorted. "Bank the forge up, Mala," he said over his shoulder. He addressed Hanno again. "No, of course not. But still, I have to make a living, don't I?"

"Of course. Any man is entitled to fair profit. So what was the Roman offering?"

"You won't believe this. Six pounds of Egyptian milled

wheat for the finished blade. I mean, I know grain prices have risen, but that's ridiculous...."

Sara had thought at first that these were social conversations. But this was the tenth or so such conversation Hanno had struck up, and she knew now how it was being shaped. She listened as a bargain was slowly forged, in a series of what sounded like general comments and complaints during a discussion of prices and the news of the day. Hanno offered his hand, and it was taken, and they left the shop.

"What's left?" he asked, once they were outside. His voice was brisker.

Sara checked her list, though she knew it well. "The Cypriot almonds..." she began.

"We'll never unload them here. Or..." Hanno's accent changed. His Greek now sounded more eastern. "...not more than a stone or two. I wouldn't even look at them."

She realized what he meant and continued to stare at her list. "I see that you're right," she confirmed, her own accent also moving eastward. She didn't turn her head. The man in the shop doorway was no doubt the same man that she had seen at the wharf when they came ashore.

"If that's all, we should go back to the ship. At least two of them promised delivery this afternoon, and we need to get our trade goods brought up on deck."

The steep little street led down to the port. Jerem was waiting with the boat, acting dumb. Literally. He could pass as an Egyptian, having the same copper skin and hooked nose as they had, and some Egyptians didn't speak Greek.

They were rowed back, passing quite close to the Roman ship on the way. A casual glance showed that of the fifteen men on its broad main deck, ten were idle, squatting, casting dice. Their hair was cut short, and they were clean-shaven. Hanno breathed only one word: "Soldiers." Sara was careful not to look.

The harbor boats came, the trade goods were cross loaded, and then they left. They had brought silver, but also tin in ingots, steel tools and weapons, fine wool, and a little gold. And fresh food.

Obala came stumping up the ladder from the hold as the sun was setting. He wiped his brow on his forearm and straightened his back. "That's the last of it," he grunted. Hanno nodded and went on watching the Roman ship. Obala followed his eye. "You're watching him; he's watching us. There's been a boat past three times this afternoon, pulling as though they've got all week, and staring at us like we was a circus act."

"I'm not surprised. You kept quiet, I suppose."

"What do you think? I had that Roman gagged, too."

Hanno frowned. "Not the best of ideas. It just about tells him that there's help not far away."

"Well, what else was I to do? If he yelled out to them . . . and in that infernal language, too . . ."

"Is he still gagged?" Sara asked urgently.

Obala blinked. "Well, I suppose . . ."

She darted below. Yes. Marcus was still gagged, tied into his hammock as if into a shroud, eyes closed and breathing noisily. Sara untied the band and allowed him to spit out the ball of rag that they'd stuffed in his mouth. It took him some time.

He glared up at her at last. "I suppose there is some explanation for this?" he demanded.

"I'm sorry. The captain thought you might make a fuss while we were away, and he was short of men to watch you. I'll get your supper now. There's fresh food." She realized that she was trying to mollify him, and she clamped her mouth shut.

"Is there, though? Well, I knew we were in a port, anyway."

Sara didn't reply. Anything she might say would give him more information, and he had probably guessed that there were Romans not far away. But not within call, or she would not have removed the gag.

She returned with a meal. It was even a proper meal. But his hands were not free, and she had to call Jerem to untie him and watch him while he ate.

"You know," he said, consideringly, "I could give my word not to attempt to escape. Nor even to call out." He munched and stared at her.

"I suppose you could." Sara attempted cool disinterest. "But would you? And would we believe you if you did?"

"Hmm. I'll think about it. I'd rather not be gagged. I've spent the last three hours trying not to throw up, in the certain knowledge that I'd drown in a spectacularly unpleasant fashion if I did."

Sara could hardly suppress a wince, but she kept her tone light. "Good. You think about it. I shall, too. Perhaps we'll come to a conclusion. No hurry, though."

She had noticed that the possibility of his word not being accepted had not occurred to Marcus. He was now thinking about something else, following on from what she'd said.

"No, there's no hurry. You'll be departing soon, anyway." He said it almost to himself.

"What makes you think that?" she asked, curious, and he looked up, exasperated.

"Really! I've been in here, swinging idly all day while sailors took most of the old cargo out and replaced it with new. Now you have a different lading, and no doubt need to go off and sell it somewhere else. Hence departure, and as soon as possible. Time is money, after all, or some such mercantile maxim." His tone was stingingly scornful.

Sara clamped down on a retort. "I couldn't say about that."

"No, I don't suppose you could."

She bit her lip again and turned to Jerem. "Let him up on deck once we've left harbor," she said.

She said nothing more, knowing that she mustn't let Marcus prod her into letting something slip. His needle was sharp, though. She watched him, saw him secure again, and climbed the ladder to the main deck. There she found Hanno and the captain.

She caught the last few words of what Hanno was saying: "...land breeze tomorrow morning."

"Most likely. But I'll need daylight to line up the leading marks, going out. We're deeper laden than we were. Good that it's mostly metal pigs, and we stowed it low. It'll make her stand up to the breeze more. Evening, miss. How's our guest?"

"Chafing, and too clever by half. Father, what are we going to do with him?"

Hanno regarded her, and for an eyeblink she thought she saw the same bleak calculation pass over his features as when he had stared at the Greek. "I've left a letter here to be sent on to a colleague in Ostia, the port for Rome itself. He, in turn, will pass it on through his own channels to the boy's father and will act as broker for the ransom."

"Marcus was saying that he thinks his father won't pay."

Hanno's eyebrows rose. "Marcus is it, now?" He considered her, while she stood her ground despite her chagrin, staring at him. Then: "Well, we'll just have to see."

But she had to know. "And if he doesn't pay, what then?"

"Well, *Marcus,* as you call him, might still come in handy. We saved his life, after all, and he might have the grace to be grateful for that." His face had become amiable, bland, somewhat like the face he had shown to the merchants in the port.

Sara still felt resentment, and she couldn't exactly say why. She glanced down the hatchway. "He doesn't have much time for traders, that's for certain," she said, testing the idea.

"Well, he wouldn't. He's what the Romans call a patrician, a member of their aristocracy. His whole class is forbidden to engage in trade or business. It would demean them, you see. The only things Roman patricians may do for a living are farming their own land or fighting."

"What?" Sara stared at her father. "That's the silliest thing I've ever heard of."

Hanno smiled vaguely. "Yes, isn't it, though? And there's worse. Romans pass their land to the eldest son only, usually. Which means that younger sons of that class—like Marcus—have only one choice in life. They can live as dependents of their father or elder brother, and under the thumb, or they can obtain land for themselves by fighting for it. That is, they must take loot and plunder, or conquer land directly."

Now his face had lost all expression. He was staring her in the eyes. "So, Rome always has a large number of influential young men who badly want a war. This might explain a lot about Rome." He nodded to the hatchway.

Sara could only blink in amazement. Strangeness. What had she said to Marcus about ways being strange? Hanno considered, then changed the subject: "We'll be off first thing in the morning. East, I think, for Alexandria, if the wind serves. That's where the metals market will be strongest, because if Rome's neighbors to the east have any brains at all, they'll be buying blades, now that the war with Carthage is over. That smith didn't know it, but Rome will certainly move against Macedonia soon." He smiled faintly. "His blades are worth more to the Macedonians than he knows."

Sara answered automatically, "But not more than you know, I see."

"No. That's because it's my business to know such things. Soon it will be yours, too. That knowledge is our living, and always was, really. I think you will carry it on, and do well." He was watching her again, assessing. Sara herself was staring at him, horrified. Her business? He saw it and smiled for an instant. "But still, give me credit. I offered the smith a fair profit, which is more than that Roman did. Everybody must profit. That's what trade is."

CHAPTER 9

Already the seamen were being roused. Sara heard movement in the cabin. Hanno was up, pulling his cloak about him. She made to rise, but he stepped between her and the pale wash of gray light coming through the curtain. "No need," he said. "There's nothing you can do on deck except get in the way. The crew is needed, so I'm going below to keep an eye on our guest. You can't help there, either. Go back to sleep, if you can." He glanced out, said something about "another hour," and stepped out on deck, pulling the curtain closed behind him.

But Sara couldn't sleep. She lay listening to low-voiced conversations on deck. A call: "Let fall!" Just after that, the ship's motion changed, and a faint groan went through her fabric. "Coming up clean." Pause. "Well enough."

Longer pause. "Anchor's aweigh!" Then came a confused medley of sounds. A rush of feet. Shouts, and in them Sara could hear genuine alarm. A sharper cry. A series of thuds. A groan.

She was on her feet before she knew it. Her own cloak had been her blanket, and now it became her cloak once again. A moment to ensure that she was decent, and she pulled the curtain aside.

There was a struggling mass of several bodies on the main deck, a pace short of the rail on the port side, and only four paces away from her. Even in the dim first light of dawn and the faint light off the sea, she could see that much but no more.

But there was her father, emerging from the hatchway in the middle of the deck. He was holding his shoulder. "Let him up," he called.

The bodies untangled themselves. Two of them, then a third. The last was still sprawled on the deck, twitching slightly.

"Get a light," said Hanno. "Don't assume he's out cold. He's probably still foxing. He foxed me nicely."

Somebody brought a lantern and handed it to him. The body on the deck was Marcus, of course. Hanno drew his foot back as if to kick, then put it down again. "Get up," he said wearily. "You're not hurt. I saw you tense."

A moment, then Marcus rose. The others stood around him. Sara saw steel glint in the lantern light.

"No," said Hanno. "Get him below again, and this time make sure he's secure. He's still worth more to us alive than dead."

Marcus smiled politely, in a deprecating sort of way. Hanno glared at him. "But not all that much more."

Hard hands gripped the Roman's arms. He was hustled below again. Sara crossed the deck. "Father?" she asked.

He rubbed his shoulder again, then flexed it in a sort of shrug. "I'm all right. Just a bruise. He came out of that hammock like a sprung cat. I had no idea he could move so fast. I thought he was asleep." Hanno looked down at the lantern still in his hand, then raised it and blew it out. He looked around at the harbor, as if seeking watchers. The Roman ship was showing a gleam, and a faint patch of light showed that her mainsail was being set. Apparently she too was making ready to sail.

Obala's head emerged from the hatch. "He's secure again now," he said, and climbed the rest of the way out. "Sorry." He seemed weary. "I was forward, making sure that anchor cable was properly hitched."

"Doing what you're supposed to be doing, you mean, while he shoved me aside and very nearly got away. If Jerem hadn't been standing there..."

"He had a nail. That's what he'd fretted his bonds away with. I think he probably kept it in his mouth."

"Clever lad." Hanno was looking up at the last fading stars. "He could have done me in, you know. There was nobody else below. He could have stabbed me with my own knife, or at least knocked me on the head. It would have improved his chances if he had."

"And also made sure we'd have killed him if we took him. It would have delayed him, anyway, so it's all one. He was just being prudent."

Sara shook her head. "Father, let me see that shoulder where there's light. And I don't think 'prudent' is a good word for him."

"No. Perhaps 'merciful' is better. A strange and non-Roman

quality. I wonder how much we may count on it, if it comes right down to it."

The morning star was disappearing already. The ship was lying parallel to a fringe of flat beach to port. Beyond the beach the land rose higher; black low hills and then, farther off, mountains could be seen, a ragged line against the stars. Out of those distant peaks, a strong cold breeze was ruffling Sara's cloak. A short half-mile ahead, a low spit loomed, with a nubble of rock along its spine, seen only because it didn't give back the faint glitter of moving water. Obala came back to the afterdeck.

"A proper land breeze, thank the gods. We'll only find the true wind when we're out to sea, but this will serve nicely for now." And, raising his voice: "Come to the wind. Broad starboard reach. Give that spit a wide berth." A bellow: "Have you got that anchor catted yet?"

The first faint flush of pink showed in the east, narrow ribbons slowly climbing up from the sea. Sara watched, turning her head, trying to take it all in: the run of the waves, the creak of ropes, the groan of timbers, the mutter of hurry, the feel of the moving ship. They slipped out, moving quickly already as the breeze took her. Soon the sea beyond the harbor mouth would be revealed. She found herself looking forward to see it stretch before her, wide, free, with the sun sparkling on it. She drew in a cool, liberating breath.

"He's slipped his mooring," said someone. "Following us out."

Sara turned to look. Yes, the Roman ship was already moving.

Obala looked sour. "This harbor's got a narrow fairway, and we're not even in it yet. We have to run out from under this point first. Then when we make the turn, both us and the Romans will have the breeze just about directly behind. I won't be able to bring the ship to the wind again until we're clear of the land."

Hanno nodded, and his brow creased, too. Sara looked up at him. "What does that mean?" she asked.

Hanno pursed his lips. "The captain is saying that we're being forced on to the only point of sailing where that Roman might be able to catch us. That is, with a strong breeze directly following. He's got a much larger mainsail, you see, and with his heavier rigging he can spread more canvas. Once we can turn across the breeze, we'll walk away from him. But until then..."

"Is he trying to catch us, though?"

"Well, there's the thing. We won't know until he actually comes alongside." He frowned again, more deeply. "But I wouldn't be surprised."

"Look there," said Obala suddenly. A sparkle reflected back from the Roman ship's deck. "Those soldiers have their armor on, anyway." He stared. "But if he was going to try something, why didn't he have a go at it last night from boats?"

Hanno shrugged. "In a friendly harbor? The war is over, we're supposed to be Rhodeans, and there might be a Roman official somewhere who'll listen to a complaint from the locals, who won't want their trade being ambushed by rogues, wherever they hail from. But once out at sea..." He brooded. "One thing, though. If he does it, he won't want anyone left to carry the tale." Silence greeted that remark. Sara felt her heart lurch. There were more than enough Roman soldiers aboard that ship to take *Heron*.

Obala was watching it come on, measuring the narrowing bearing with his eye.

"Well, he's going to come close," he remarked eventually. "I think we'll make the turn for the outer road only about a cable in front of him." Then he shook his head. "But all the same, it's no go for him. Close is not good enough. He's a real slug. I don't think he even knows how a proper sea boat will handle." He turned. "Deck, there! When I go about, quick's the word and sharp's the action, d'ye hear me?"

They would have had to be as deaf as posts not to. Obala motioned for the tillerman to edge a little more away. "We're shaving the edge of the shoal," he said. They waited. The sun peered over the hills that fringed the harbor. Both vessels seemed to be making for the same point on the green water, but Sara could now see that *Heron* would reach it first. It was like a race, the foam flying and the wind keen and brisk, with an urgent chuckle at the cutwater. The breeze was still blowing cool and strong out of the Spanish mountains, enough to send her hair streaming in tendrils across her face, and the lift of the sea and the sudden return of light to the world exhilarated her in a way that almost shocked her. It made her catch her breath, the sheer brilliant delight of it. She had never thought she would feel this way again. She almost cried aloud as the bow flung a sharp shower of spray aft, the shock sparkling on her face.

They made the turn only a long bowshot in front of the

Roman. Obala volleyed orders, and the yard swung around until it was almost exactly square with the line of the deck. He tested the strength of the breeze and shook his head. "Too much for the topsail," he remarked. "Maybe when we reach the true wind." He swung around and stared at the oncoming bow of the Roman ship. "But even at this, we're holding our own. Once we're clear of the land, we'll run right away from that tub."

"He's cracking on. There—he's setting his own topsail."

Obala only shook his head again. "Let him. With a hull like that, in this breeze, it'll only press her down. In half an hour we'll be out of the roads and free to turn across the wind. It's already got some west in it." He eyed the distance again. "I think we're gaining, even now."

It seemed that they were. It took some time for the change to become apparent, but the blocky hull and vast mainsail of the Roman ship slowly receded. But it took until nearly noon before it was far enough off and the land no more than a faint shadow on the horizon.

"I think this is the true breeze now," said Obala. "Nor' wester. Looks like it might be strengthening, even. But if we want to lose that lubber, we'd best put it on our starboard quarter and run south for the deep water. We can turn east again once we've sunk his masthead. Any storm will come out of the west, anyway, and we might as well have the sea room to run before it, if need be."

"As you say, Captain. You know your ship—"

A long, wailing hail from the masthead interrupted Hanno. "Deck! Galley! One point abaft the weather beam, and running down!" Sara found herself understanding. An oared galley was to windward, making speed toward them. She felt a sudden cold jolt, like a chilled iron spike in the belly.

Obala gasped, called on the gods, spun on his heel, and was down the ladder to the main deck and halfway up the weather shrouds faster than Sara had believed a man of his size could move. He twisted to stare for a moment, then barked a word she had never heard in her life, before he began bellowing orders. "Come about! Wear ship! Hard over! Hands to the braces! Hands to the goddamn braces, I said, blast you! Abar, wake that staring nitwit up! Get the wind broad on her port quarter. Haul that yard around, gods damn you all. Heave! Heave for your lives!" He was already springing up the ladder to the afterdeck again.

To Hanno: "Damn it to hell and back! I can't come onto the starboard reach. He'll just run down and snap us up. We'll have to pass his bow and get to windward of him. But the land isn't far the other way."

Hanno nodded. "You think that galley's a pirate, then?"

"A fifty-oared galley? In these waters? What else can he be? He was waiting for us, blast him, to windward of the harbor entrance. And gods damn him, the land's ahead now. If he can find a little more speed, he'll pinch us up against it, and we'll either be taken or hit the rocks."

Minutes passed, fleeting away while they watched the agonizingly slow relative movement of the ships. And yet *Heron* was sailing fast, leaning far over. The spray from the weather bow was being flung aft in stinging sheets as the ship shouldered into the steep little seas. It seemed a long time, but at last Hanno sighed, and Sara knew it was with relief. "We seem to be doing well enough," he said, turning to the captain, and Obala nodded, his eyes closing.

Even Sara could see it, a few minutes later. They were appreciably crossing the galley's course now, moving upwind of him.

"He won't get us on this reach. Thank the gods for a stiff breeze," said Obala. "He hadn't counted on that. He's got oars, but he's still making a lot more leeway than us. That's a galley for you—they go to leeward like a raft, once the wind gets up."

"The land's coming up fast. We'll have to turn soon."

Obala grimaced. "One thing at a time. If we leave the turn for the last moment, we'll give ourselves more chance...huh?"

The last sound was a grunt of pure surprise. Obala shook water out of his eyes and looked again. "He's turning downwind himself. Oh..."

"The Roman," said Hanno flatly. "He can't work to weather like we can, and he looks the richer prize. The galley will have him."

They watched. The Roman ship held her course, sagging down to leeward as the pirate came up. Obala shook his head. "The Roman's holding on, for god's sake. He'd make it a lot longer chase, at least, if he put the wind directly behind. What in Baal's own furnace is he thinking of? There's fifty or more of them bastards aboard the galley. Soldiers or no soldiers, he's..."

"I'll tell you what he's thinking. He's thinking he's a Roman."

A different voice. Flat, certain. Marcus had come on deck.

He was bound, unshaven, and barefoot. Jerem stood beside him, intercepting the captain's basilisk glare. Sara stared, too, but it was to her that Jerem spoke: "Sorry, miss. You told me to let him walk on deck. I didn't know about all this. . . ." He gestured around.

Jerem had been watching the Roman captive since long before daylight. Sara had meant to relieve him. "Oh . . . I'm so sorry, Jerem. Someone should have . . ." She switched to Greek to address Marcus. "You'll have to go below. . . ."

Marcus gestured with his bound hands. "Look! Someone just flashed a legionary shield on the foredeck where the pirate can't see it through the sail. That's Seventh Apulia, or I'm an Etruscan. Demobilized legion from the war in Spain, most likely, heading home."

"She isn't carrying more than fifteen or twenty of them. There's fifty or sixty men in that galley," said Obala flatly.

"Do you think that matters? He's a Roman." Marcus jerked his head toward the galley. "That's a pirate. Orders are to suppress piracy. So that's what he'll do." Marcus paused. "He's counting on us to help him. And we can do this, between us."

Obala seemed to swell with indignation. "What do you mean, *we, us,* and *help*? Let him suppress his pirate, if that's what he wants, and it's the far horizons for us."

Marcus was shaking his head. "Take another look, Captain. Look how we lie. There's the land. We're embayed. The galley can carry that ship, and then wait for us to turn across him again. We either help, or risk getting snapped up piecemeal. And any decent seaman, even a merchant, should help another against a pirate."

Silence. The captain's head turned, looking at the galley, looking at the Roman ship, looking at the nearing land. Sara stepped away. She had Aram's little knife in the cabin, she remembered. She turned to go down.

And halted again. On the main deck, a minor struggle was going on. Jerem was pulling at Marcus's shoulder, and Marcus was resisting.

"No!" He pushed his bound hands out, pleading, in the direction of the afterdeck. "Let me help. Give me my gear. I'm one more man. I'll...I'll give my word. I won't escape. I will wait to be ransomed." A struggle showed on his face. "More. I'll go parole for you. I'll tell the commander to let you go."

The captain drew breath in, presumably to bellow, but Hanno stepped in front of him. "Why would you do that?" he asked mildly, leaning on the afterdeck rail, looking down at Marcus. It sounded as though he were enquiring about the price of olives.

Marcus stared at him. "I owe you my life. Those are Romans over there." He shook his head, imploring. "My duty is to help them. I'll do what I must to persuade you to let me. My father would approve, if he knew."

"Indeed. And if we are persuaded, what then? We'd have to trust your word."

"Even if you didn't, how would you be worse off? Those pirates will simply cut everyone's throat. And I'll tell you straight, if that fellow outranks me"—he nodded at the Roman ship—"or if he's just not willing to listen, it might be no good anyway. But I swear that I'll do my best to get you off, and I won't escape myself. I swear it by my lares and penates."

"Ah," said Hanno. He seemed to consider.

"He swears by what?" asked Sara.

"His household gods," replied Hanno shortly. Then he nodded. "All right. Loose him. Give him his armor and weapons." He shot a glance at the captain, and there was a moment of balance as Obala seemed to hesitate. He was reading Hanno's face.

Then the captain's pent breath exploded in orders. "Do it! And get weapons, all of you. Move!"

Jerem waited just a moment longer, until he saw Sara's confirming nod. Then he stepped back. Marcus held up his hands. A blur in the air, and the cords were cut.

"Where is my sword and armor?" Jerem dived down the hatchway, and Marcus followed him.

"Father," asked Sara, "why?"

Hanno's face didn't change. "It improves our chances, which is always a sound principle. And I really think he's right. The pirates might have taken the Roman by then and be able to take us as well. More important, it makes a Roman—two Romans, in fact—into our debtors. We may be able to turn a profit from that." He watched the ships, calculating. "You'd better go into the cabin."

"No, I'd better not. I'll stay here. I'll need to know what's happening."

He might have been about to make a sharp answer, demanding obedience, but the calm certainty of her voice reproved him. He frowned, but her face didn't change. She simply returned his regard. After a moment, he shook his head and looked away. "At least go down to the main deck, where you'll be in some cover," he said. "They'll be shooting shortly, and we can't shoot back. You'll see just as well from there. Please."

Sara wondered whether she should defy that as well. "If you come, too," she said. He hesitated, and she took his hand. "You can't do anything by standing here, either," she added, and after a moment he complied, descending the steep little steps. Here the break of the afterdeck covered them. They crouched in its shadow.

"They'll board over the Roman's weather side," shouted the captain. "Get ready."

The pirates were shooting now from their galley, trying to discourage intervention. Two archers stood on its scrap of foredeck, balancing against the roll. Most of their shots were aimed at the Roman ship, but a sharp thud announced the arrival of at least one arrow aboard the *Heron*. It had buried its head in the afterdeck rail, not more than an arm's length from the captain, as he stood braced at the tiller. He ignored it. Another shaft skimmed low over the deck.

A steel gleam rose out of the hatchway. A spearhead appeared, then a helmet, and then the top of the Roman shield, a long oval that covered a man from his throat to his calf. Marcus climbed to the main deck, saw the arrow's flight, and ran up to the tiller. He put his shield between the captain and the galley. A moment later, another arrow cracked into it, like death knocking.

Jerem also emerged from the hatchway, climbing awkwardly, one-handed. Under his arm was a bundle of short throwing spears. Roman spears, the ones harvested from the last encounter. He stood by the steps, ready to pass them to Marcus.

Marcus was eyeing the galley. Again an arrow thudded against his shield, but this one glanced off. He watched the sea, flexing his knees, letting the heave of the deck become part of him.

"We're a much more stable platform than that craft," he remarked comfortably, as though discussing the weather. "We don't seem to roll as much."

"That's a galley for you. Shallow draft. Not much more than an open boat, that one. Rolls on a millpond, but the wind helps to keep us steady," said the captain. "Now, listen. We're upwind, which means we can choose when we approach them. I'm holding off until they're stuck into your friends there. But the wind's against their arrows and it's with your javelins."

Marcus nodded. He watched the archers on the galley's foredeck. One was drawing, the other reaching for another shaft. The oars beat, up, down, up, as *Heron* closed. A point arrived that Marcus seemed to recognize. He drew back a pace. As both archers fitted arrow on string, he stepped forward, his fingers twining the leather thong to spin the spear. He twisted, then uncoiled like a snake striking. His whole body flung itself after his shoulder and arm.

The spear arced out of Sara's sight. But there was an agonized shriek, and her blood ran cold. Obala shouted. Marcus grunted, caught the next spear that Jerem tossed to him, and fell back on guard again.

"Missed him," said Marcus. "Low and right. I only hit his leg." He seemed to think that this was a failure. Sara stared up at him. His face had taken on the cold remoteness of a statue's. "The other one's flung himself flat."

"Wise of him, but he can't shoot like that."

"Yes. No use trying for him, or for the rowers. I can only see the tops of their heads. And the helmsman is still out of throwing range."

"He won't be for long. They're coming alongside the Roman now." Hanno was trying to see around the shield and the armored figure.

"Do you need to see better, Captain?" Marcus's words came with a studied, almost drugged calm. Sara wondered how he did it. She felt her heart pounding, her stomach twisting. The galley's prow came into sight past the ledge of the afterdeck, and she pressed back against the bulwark.

"I can see the galley well enough," replied Obala. He shouted: "Deck, there. They aren't shooting anymore. Stand by to shorten sail when I put the helm over." A shrill whine ended in a sharp crack against Marcus's shield. "Bloody hell. What was that?"

"Sling bullet," replied Marcus briefly. "They can use a sling sitting down."

"Huh. See if you can pin their helmsman when we hit."

Marcus nodded, calm as a stone. Obala shifted his attention back to the galley.

"I might hit him now," said Marcus. The voice was a cool assessment of chances, dispassionate as a balance sheet.

"Wait...wait." Obala's burred voice had dropped to a

croon. Another slingstone rapped the Roman's shield, and a second rang off his helmet with a buzz like a passing wasp. Marcus didn't seem to notice it.

The galley's prow was coming level with the Roman's cutwater, but the pirate craft was longer and lower. It would range up, grapple, and pull the two together. Then there'd be a wave of boarders that could never be held on the thinly manned bulwarks. The oars beat, once more, twice more. There was the beginning of a rumble.

"He's boating oars. Now!" Obala hauled on the rudder, and the sail was shortened, men hauling on the lines like demons. *Heron* turned downwind, toward the galley. And Marcus threw.

The galley was alongside the Roman ship now. Rowers sprang up from the benches and grabbed for weapons. Others heaved grapnels, and the two vessels were pulled into a deadly embrace.

In the same moment, Marcus grunted in satisfaction. Again Sara heard that terrible bubbling shriek.

"They can't say they haven't been kissed, anyway," said Marcus calmly. He hefted another spear. "And there we are. Those legionnaires have been below to tempt that pirate to come in. Look—they're boiling up out of the hatches now. Ave, Apulia! Venio!" The last was a bark that might have been heard across the waters.

The captain grinned. "Well, they can at least keep them busy while we run for..." He bit the words off. Marcus had turned his head and was staring at him, and in his face was the same calm assessment as when he had speared the archer. "Joke. Just a joke. I'm running in now. See?"

For the first time, the galley seemed to pause. Its crew hesitated. Nobody seemed to be in charge. Perhaps the helmsman Marcus had struck had been the captain. Over a general hubbub, shouts could be heard, several voices, alarmed at the sight of the wave of armed and armored Roman soldiers pouring up onto the ship's deck. Steel twinkled. A bellowed order, and the Roman shields locked together, like the stones of a wall.

Now the galley had stopped pulling, her oars trailing in the water. Roman javelins were flying. As the metal-tipped rain fell among the pirates, *Heron* ranged up on her other side. With a crunch she smacked into the portside bank of oars. Again grapnels flew, and the sides locked together. A shout from the Romans, and the solid clump of shields had stepped over the galley's low bulwark. But it was a small clump, and a much larger crowd of armed men ranged against it, pressing it against the side.

"Fifteen. Only fifteen of them. Come on. We're needed. Every man." Marcus ran down the main deck and along the starboard side, passing Sara and Hanno without a glance. The seamen gathered behind him. Maro, Aram's groom, had found his cavalry helmet and his shield. Jerem stood to the other side.

The pirates were mostly facing away, and they were all yelling. Some saw *Heron* coming in but didn't immediately realize that the situation had reversed—that the hunted had become the hunters—and those who did realize it had no time to warn others. Marcus cheered and leaped across, and the others followed him, a yelling wave of men.

The galley's afterdeck was deserted as every man of her

crew rallied to the fight amidships, where the Roman line was still holding but hardly moving. Obala secured a line to the sternpost, then launched himself across to the galley's afterdeck. For a moment he seemed to be trailing the rope in the air behind him like a monkey its tail. He landed, stumbled forward, braced himself, and hauled in. Now all three vessels lay side by side, rocking on the low swell.

Sara, desperate to see, turned and climbed up on the weather rail, standing on it, holding the shrouds. Now she could see the whole business. The Romans had formed their shields into the same impenetrable wall that she had seen before, but now there was a solid hedge of them, not just three men fighting back-to-back. Between the shields, a flicker of steely gleams showed—the Roman short swords, stabbing. They were holding their ground, no more, striving to go forward but pressed hard.

Suddenly Sara realized. She knew that this was what Aram had seen and what he had heard in the last hour of his life. The agony and the blood. The shouts and the sudden wordless shrieks, the melee that seemed formless until you saw it from above. She climbed higher, unconscious of what she was doing.

It gained a pattern—a grim, solid Roman line that moved together as one, a step at a time, grinding against the swirling mass of the pirates that confronted it in a swinging, slashing, yelling crowd. But behind the pirates, biting into them, was the wedge whose point was Marcus Licinius Corbo. When the line and the wedge met, the pirate mass would be split apart like a melon under a blade.

And the wedge was making progress, slicing into the

crowd from behind. Maro chopped with his long cavalry sword, and a man staggered back, blood pouring from his neck. Another bowed suddenly to Jerem, choking, holding his belly, and then fell sideways, kicking, a frightful glimpse of ropy intestines spilling. Sara felt the cold clutch of horror. She tore her gaze away, toward Marcus as he stabbed, slammed his shield into an astonished face, stepped over a body, ducked, and stabbed again, an explosion of purposeful, applied violence that was as appalling in itself. Now pirates were turning, trying to face in two directions as the attacks converged. The Roman line surged as the pressure came off it. It took a single definite step forward. Another.

And suddenly it was over. The line and the wedge joined. The crowd fragmented, lost cohesion, tore into rags. Pirates started diving overboard, casting away weapons and striking out for the shore a long mile away. Others stayed and died. The last minute was hideous beyond anything so far, for no quarter was given pirates, wounded or hale. Sara turned her face away and stared out across the clean sea, until it was over.

She descended, concentrating hard on the lines of the planking, thinking about where to set her feet, what to hold on to. Not listening. Not seeing, as if she could separate herself from it by not acknowledging the horrors going on only twenty paces away.

She reached the rail, then the deck. She looked around to find Hanno, to tell him about what she'd seen and understood. To comfort him, and to seek comfort.

He wasn't there. She couldn't see him. Where ...?

They were calling her from the other side. She looked up sharply, half looking for him, half answering them.

But she saw nothing. The galley's side was lower. She couldn't see half of it from here. There were bodies. . . . Where was Hanno? Where was her father?

Jerem, blood on his hands, blood on his tunic, came leaping up over the rail. "You better come, miss," he said. And then he looked away, not meeting her eyes. "You better come quick."

CHAPTER 10

It was a belly wound. She had sniffed at it, as her mother had taught her. It was clean. She was sure. She had sutured, cauterized, and bandaged it, slowing the bleeding and closing the layers of muscle, layers that had failed to protect the vulnerable viscera inside. But she was sure it was clean. The clutch of fear, the shivering icy dismay in her own stomach—that could be ignored. It must be ignored.

Hanno had stood it well enough. He could hardly speak, for the drawing of breath was agonizing. She packed him around in the cot with padded canvas, to limit the movement caused by the ship's motion, working slowly, carefully, not accepting assistance. Finally she stood back and stared down at him. The others traded glances, shifting on their feet. Marcus cleared his throat.

She answered without looking around. "Yes, yes, all right. I'm coming."

The shore was close. They had to get the ships away from

it, out into the open sea, but there were explanations to make, wounded to be tended.

Three more of *Heron*'s crew were wounded, and six of the Romans too, despite their mail shirts, helmets, and shields. Going across to the other ship, Sara wondered how they had come off so lightly. The galley was littered with corpses. She looked away, sickened, as the men stripped it—there were valuables aboard, she heard—fired it and pushed it off downwind. The hull burned on the rolling sea, and Sara was deeply grateful for the clean wind that pushed the galley away toward Africa with her cargo of death.

She stitched, clamped, and bandaged, working on the Roman deck, demanding coldness of herself. One soldier had been struck by a sling bullet just below the elbow of the sword arm. One of the lower arm bones was broken, and she set and splinted it, using Jerem to haul the bone into place. Another had a deep slash to the upper arm. Both soldiers simply stared at the sky as she worked, as if they were not present at all. The same for the painful business of stitching a scalp wound. The Roman soldier sat without moving a muscle while she did it, said what might have been words of thanks, and then rose and walked away without a tremor.

She was finishing with the last of them and listening to Marcus interviewing the man who commanded them. Apparently the latter was a minor officer, a file leader or something. Marcus had addressed him as "*ordile.*" They were both standing on the deck, easily within earshot as she worked.

She was listening, but she had no idea what they were saying. The language was strange to her. Question from the under officer; decisive answer from Marcus. Then what might have been a tentative objection, to be met by a patient sigh and a slightly longer reply. A gesture indicated Sara, tending the Roman wounded. The underofficer looked but shrugged slightly.

He seemed to be about to say more, but something odd happened. Marcus reached up and scratched his nose. The under officer's eyes seemed drawn to his hand. A moment later the soldier straightened his shoulders and stiffened into immobility. Then, with a crisp slap of palm on chest, the under officer turned smartly, snapped a command to his men, and stepped back. Marcus nodded politely, put his hands behind his back, and sauntered over to Sara.

"Are you finished?" he asked.

She nodded, repacking her bag. "For now," she said. "I'm not sure about that broken arm. And at least two of them will need a competent surgeon."

"They'll get one. He's running into Saguntum. And he's letting us go. On my say-so, but I'd recommend not giving him a lot of time to think about it. Just as well his employer, the owner of this tub, had the misfortune to get in the way of a javelin. He's their only fatality."

She nodded and rose. She was desperate to get back. Then something in his tone registered, despite the weariness and the chilling anxiety. "A javelin? But...only you Romans were throwing javelins."

His face had gone perfectly blank. "No doubt one of the pirates picked one up. Shame, really. The ordile explained that the orders he had been given—to board and take *Heron*—were perfectly illegal, the war being over, and he had protested them. As he put it, he wasn't going to turn pirate himself, and once it became clear that there was a Roman citizen aboard *Heron,* that more or less sealed it. No doubt there would have been some sort of trial later. But now the man is dead, so neither the ordile nor I will be put to the trouble of bringing a charge."

She stared at him. His hands had locked behind his back, and he stared back at her without expression. "You'll be going with them, of course," she said after a moment, and then she had to wonder why she felt an obscure dismay.

Marcus's eyes opened wider, and his face changed. Now he looked as though she had suggested that he grow wings and fly back to Rome. "Of course *not.* I swore I wouldn't escape, by my household gods. I could never show my face at home again, if I forswore myself. My father would kill me. What do you take me for?" He took her elbow. "Shall we go?" She was so astonished that she went without a murmur.

The captain looked up as they arrived on *Heron*'s deck. "Can we part company now?" he asked. "The longer we stay hove-to like this, the more we go downwind."

Marcus smiled slightly. "Certainly, Captain. Set sail at once, or whatever you do." And to Sara: "Smile," he said. "Wave. You're under Rome's protection now."

Sara pulled her arm away. "Smile? Wave? Are you mad? Get out of my way!" She thrust him aside and ran for the cabin, staggering slightly as the sail filled with a crack and *Heron* leaned over to the wind.

Hanno hadn't changed. He was still lying rigid in the cot, knees slightly drawn up, breathing shallowly, his eyes half-closed. She felt his scalp. A slight fever was only to be expected at this stage, she told herself. . . .

"I'm sorry. I was congratulating myself on my diplomatic skills, and I forgot myself. I beg your pardon. How is he?"

Marcus stood in the frame of the door. She forced herself to answer. "About the same." And then, with sick dread, "We won't know for a day or two."

It was the truth. All might yet be well. She had to tear her mind away from the other possibility. "What did you say to him? The Roman on the other ship?"

"I just told him that this ship wasn't out of Carthage last, wasn't carrying contraband, wasn't an enemy of Rome—why, look at how we'd fought for Rome and how you were tending his men—and anyway was transporting a Roman."

"The best lies are entirely true in themselves," Sara whispered, and thought she saw an answering gleam in Hanno's half-closed eyes.

"Exactly." Marcus appeared to think she was paying him a compliment.

"And did that convince him?"

A deprecating gesture. "He might have gotten the impression that my journey was entirely voluntary. Even, perhaps, that there was some official color to it. I told him I couldn't discuss it with a legionary decurion. Naturally, he took that for confirmation."

"Hmm. He certainly seemed to get the message very suddenly. Sprang to attention, for some reason, stopped asking questions, slapped his chest. All but started bowing and scraping."

"Oh, no, he wouldn't have done that. He's a freeborn Roman citizen, just like me."

Sara heard the falseness in the tone, just the faintest touch of smugness. "But not just like you, it seems."

"Well...not quite the same. He might have noticed this." Marcus held his left hand up. A dull-gray, plain metal band circled the ring finger.

Sara had noticed it before. "I thought that was odd," she said. "Was it supposed to be silver but turned out to be mostly lead? A gift from a...a lady, perhaps?"

"Ah...no. It's iron, very pure so it doesn't rust. And it's not exactly a gift."

"An iron ring? How odd." She spoke absently. Water. Hanno would not be able to drink for days. A soaked cloth should be arranged to trickle water into his mouth....

"I suppose so. It's worn by Roman patricians. Those whose ancestors have served in the Roman magistracies and were seated in the Senate. And not all of those, either. Only the oldest families still wear the iron ring."

His voice had become almost meditative. Sara felt her eyebrows rise. "Ah," she said. "Most impressive."

His eyes shifted to her face. "Well, it is. The Licinii have been patricians of Rome for over two hundred years."

"Oh? And what were they before that?"

Marcus blinked in confusion. "Well, uh...it's said that—"

"Said? Don't you *know*?"

"Um. Well, not...I mean...how could anyone go that far back...?"

"How? Why, by writing it down, of course. We have ancestral records going back over five hundred years...at home."

Her voice dropped on the last words. Home. They might never go home again, and all the records would be lost. Sara forced the thought away, just as she had forced other thoughts away, and folded her arms. "I can tell you all about my twelve-times great-grandfather. His name, his rank, what he did, his services to the city, his offices, his distinctions, his donations," she said. "But no matter. You were saying about your own...um...distinguished family?"

Marcus was blinking. Then he took a breath and almost spoke, and it might have been angrily. But he looked at her face first, and after a moment, he held up a hand. "Your hit, as we say. Consider me well put in my place. My father would be laughing, if he ever laughed." He shook his head. "Mind you, it wouldn't change his mind. Nothing ever changes his mind, once he's made it up."

Sara said nothing further. She pulled up a stool and began the vigil. Her father's face had not changed. *Heron* moved out to sea.

Hanno was worse the following day, and worse the day after. By the third, with the wound discharging a stinking greenish ooze, it was clear that he was dying.

He hadn't spoken. Sara could only change the dressing. She had already inserted a straw to help the wound drain, but she could see now that the seat of the evil was too deep. It was far inside the belly, beyond her medicine, beyond her skill. She had used half her small stock of poppy syrup, and now she knew she must reserve the rest for a single massive dose, enough to ease him away on its wings.

It was taking him quickly now. His flesh had shrunk away from his bones until he was a racked husk of a man. He was breathing in shallow, agonized pants. She must decide. Soon he would be unable to swallow. If she was to give him surcease, it must be soon.

She turned from the bed and opened her medicine chest. The tightly stoppered flask came into her hand, and she lifted it out, unable to see now, blinded with the tears, her throat convulsing. Her hands must not shake, though. She would not allow it.

She poured it out into a cup and diluted it with just enough wine to make it easier to swallow. Yet even this was not sure. Nothing was sure. Poppy was fickle. It might be enough to send him into sleep, and then bring a gentle death. It might make little difference. It might only prolong it. She didn't know.

A shadow fell over her. Jerem. He had been coming and going, taking out the foul cloths, replacing them, sitting with her when she'd fallen asleep for a while. He saw her take the flask, and he knew what it meant, and he bowed his head.

But she could not do it. She could not. She rocked backward and forward on the stool, arms clenched to her sides, head bowed over the cup.

"That's his medicine, is it, miss?" asked Jerem.

The cup was shaking in her grasp. She clutched it with both hands, steadying it. She could not answer.

"I'll give it to him, miss, shall I?"

She shook her head. She could not. She must, but she could not.

And Hanno's eyes opened. He looked up at Jerem. He had been racked with fever, but this was the last stage, when his body had no more strength left to fight, and the fever was fitful now. His hand twitched, and Jerem nodded. "Right you are, sir."

He took the cup gently out of Sara's hands, and she gave

it up without a struggle, grateful that it was being done. He supported the head of Hanno Harcar, and held the cup to his lips. Hanno drank, drank again, swallowed painfully, drank again.

The cup was empty. Jerem gently lowered Hanno's head.

"Sara." A faint whisper. "Go now." He looked up at Jerem. "Now."

"Yes, sir."

"Father...why did you do it? Why did you go to fight?" Sobs were racking her. She choked the words, but he understood.

"Even a merchant...even a merchant..." he whispered. The drug was taking him, his breathing slowing, something like a relaxing coming over his rigid limbs. "Trust Marcus. Roman...client...debt..." and something more, but it was lost. Then one more word, a single breath: "Now." The eyes closed.

"Yes, sir," said Jerem. He looked up. "I'll do what's needful."

He was speaking to Marcus, who stood in the doorframe. Marcus must have understood, for he nodded. He stooped and raised Sara to her feet. "He'll sleep now. Come," he said.

She was already standing. Her father had said, "Go now." Marcus's arm was around her, and his voice was sure, certain and commanding. She had slept three hours in the last three days. A protest came automatically to her lips, but he ignored it, and she had no strength to resist.

On deck, the sun made shafts of gold among clouds that trailed silver veils of rain. Shadows of sail and rigging moved gently back and forth across the pitching deck. The ship heaved easily under her, and far off, a green coast with dim blue hills behind it rose out of the white-rippled sea. She felt the caress of the wind and the kiss of the sun and thought, How beautiful, how beautiful.

Marcus's arm tightened around her shoulders. She turned her head, and, as she expected, Jerem had come out of the cabin. His eyes met those of Marcus, then hers.

"It's over, miss," he said. "He's gone. It was very, very quick, at the end. He didn't suffer at all."

A corpse is an unlucky thing to have aboard a ship. He must be slipped over the side as soon as possible. Long before Sara was capable of thought or movement, they had sewn him into canvas with iron billets at his feet. Sara kissed him and bound the head cloth that shrouded him. She knew not to inspect his body further. It would be disrespectful. He had said, "Now."

They carried him out on a plank, rested one end on the rail, and the captain brought the ship to the wind, giving them a lee. She had no petals to strew, no sacrifice to make. She could only offer Baal of the Oceans her tears and hope that their tiny addition to his vast domain would please him. The men raised the end of the plank, and the body of Hanno Harcar, late senator of Carthage, slid over the side and disappeared into the curling sea.

CHAPTER 11

She slept. Sleep had ambushed her. Her father and brother came to her in her dreams, and they seemed happy. She woke, aching and weeping.

Daylight showed through the drawn curtain. She had been aware of it for some time before she could think about anything and before the acute misery began once more. She tried to escape into sleep again, but her body's needs were urgent and they drove her to the necessary, a scuttle by the after bulkhead. As she moved, she heard Obala—not exactly his voice, but a curious, strangulated half-whispered shadow of it—ordering the topsail be taken in.

The ship's motion had changed. *Heron* was moving smoothly, a long corkscrewing roll, and deep. Sara's thoughts moved slowly, searching for meaning. The sea must be getting up. The curtain across the doorway was tautly toggled on both sides, but it rippled and quivered. A strong breeze was blowing, clearly.

She dry-scrubbed her face with the palms of her hands.

Her eyes were gummy, and she felt grimy. Her thoughts trudged their weary round again. They had buried her father yesterday. She had not been able to save him.

Some level of her mind still functioned. There was a bucket with water, enough for a wash. When she was finished, it had to be carried out. She pulled two of the toggles through their loops, the curtain flapped wildly, and she pulled it aside.

It was early morning. She couldn't recall going to sleep. That must have been yesterday. She stood for a moment in the opening. Two seamen who were scrubbing the deck with holystones sprang up when they saw her. One kicked over his bucket, and it rolled across the planking, rattling.

Another strangled whisper came from behind and above her. "Gods blast and damn you, you clumsy sod, if you've woken her I'll..." Scuffling footsteps sounded on the upper deck. Obala was apparently walking on tiptoe. He came to the upper-deck rail and saw her standing below him. "Oh. Morning, miss. Did these...people disturb you?" His normal voice had returned.

She shook her head, looking up at him. "No. I was awake." The sun was rising to port, to the leeward side. Unasked, her mind performed the calculations. That would mean that they were headed roughly south, and the wind was from the west, or a bit north of it. It was blowing steady, fresh, and strong.

She went to the lee rail and emptied the bucket over the side. There was only one jut of land in sight now, and it was well astern, to the north of them. Was that Spain? Gaul? Serdana? Some other island? She didn't know.

As automatically, she returned the bucket, secured the

curtain, and climbed the steps to the afterdeck. Obala was standing by the rail. He stepped aside for her.

"What's that land?" she asked.

"That's the southern point of Serdana, miss. Wind's been a lot kinder to us than on the voyage out. Fresh breezes, never heading us. We'll be home in a day or two."

Sara shook her head. Home? "We're going back home? To Carthage?" she asked.

"Yes, of course, miss."

She forced herself to concentrate. "Ah. Ah, no. That's not right."

"Miss?"

She struggled with the notion. "That's not where we're going. Father…the senator said we should go to Alexandria." What was left to go home to, anyway? What had happened to Carthage? She didn't know.

Obala was smiling, reassuring. "Oh. Well, no disrespect to the senator, but I don't think so now, miss. I've got to get you back to someone who'll look after you. You'll have relatives…someone…in Carthage. The Romans haven't sacked the city, they said. It'll be all right."

She was staring at him. "Relatives?" Her numb mind sorted through memories, faces, a past that was distant and almost alien, seen as if through turbulent water. "I've got cousins, if they're not dead." She had, too. The three daughters of Father's deceased elder brother, all running households of their own, and they'd have to take her in, if they were indeed living. Yrta, Salome, and Jara. Yrta was very pious, Salome was house-proud and a terror to her servants, and Jara was a drudge with no conversation at all, not even about her seven children. But, yes, they'd have to take her in. Grudgingly, no doubt, but...

And then she looked around her at the swooping deck, the green and marching sea, and felt the keen clear air on her face. What the captain was saying suddenly blazed into meaning. And now he was speaking again: "There you are, then. Best we take you back and get you settled as soon as we can."

Sara could only shake her head and grope for words. Again she looked around at the sea, open, free. At least she had managed a great house, before. If she became a dependent on a cousin, she could expect to be treated as a servant and married off as soon as possible to anyone who'd have her. "Back? No. No, that isn't possible. I can't go back." As soon as she said it, she realized it was true. She couldn't; she could never go back. But the captain was shaking his head.

"Never mind, miss. Don't worry about it. The war's over now." He half turned away.

"No. No, listen to me. Listen to me!" She had swung around on him, and the sudden snap in her voice pulled him up short. He stared at her in surprise. "The senator said Alexandria. He said that for a reason." But she didn't know what that reason was....

Wait a moment. He had said..."It's the best place to sell the cargo. Silver bars. Alexandria is the market for them, he said."

The captain was shaking his head. "There's a silver market in Carthage," he said, soothing, calming. "I'll get you a fair price, don't you worry."

She found herself beginning to shake with anger. But

it was no use blazing out at him. He'd just put it down to female hysteria, then refuse to listen at all. She had to think. Think! Silver. What was it Father had said about silver? That Carthage needed it, but perhaps too much? What had he meant by that?

There was no time. The captain was just about to turn away again, dismissing her, sure of his rightness. She had to shake him out of it. What had Father meant? Shouldn't you take goods to where they were wanted? But no, that wasn't the only thing. You took them to where they could be traded for a profit.

"No, no. You don't understand. Silver bullion. Silver..." Under the desperate prodding, her mind was moving again, coming alive. They'd need the silver too much! "The city's desperate for it, to pay off the Romans, but...but..." And then it came to her. "They've nothing to trade for it. The port's been idle for months. They'll have to call in every debt they own, but that'll take years." She followed her thought, not knowing as she spoke where it would lead. "If they need it so badly, they'd probably...yes! They'd probably—what-do-you-call-it—requisition our silver for, I don't know, a promissory note, or maybe...maybe they'd just confiscate it outright!" Her mouth dropped open. She saw the consternation on the captain's face, and she followed up. "Yes. It makes sense. Father had enemies. Necessity knows no law." She thought about it and realized that what she was saying was actually true. "That's what they really would do. Father...the senator knew that. *That's* why he said to make for Alexandria."

But the captain was frowning and still shaking his head.

"Well, I don't know about that...I really can't say, I'm sure...but you must let me worry about it. I'll do right by you, I promise. You don't need to bother your head..."

But her mind was racing on. "And we're carrying sword blades and steel bars, too." She thought about that, about sailing into Carthage harbor with them aboard, and suddenly the implication hit her like a blow. She gasped. "The Romans—they'll still be there! It'll take months for them to get their army away, tens of thousands of men. They'll be camped around the city, if they're not actually in it, and they'll certainly control the harbor. Why...why..." She stared at him in shock. "Good gods, man, do you realize what they'll do if they catch a ship running *weapons* into Carthage?"

At last she had reached him. The captain's face blanched. His mouth opened. He almost staggered. Then he looked down at the hatchway into the hold. "Them blades are stowed low, of course," he muttered after a moment. He looked around at the heaving water. "I can't rummage the hold to come at them, not in this sea...."

Sara realized that he was actually considering heaving them overboard. She gasped at the sheer blank stupidity of it.

"No. No. You mustn't think of it. We'll run them into Alexandria. Father dealt with..." She racked her brains again, flitting through memories, half-forgotten conversations, something Aram had told her once..."the Maimonii. He always said they were honest. And he expected to turn a good profit on the steel there."

Obala scowled, shifting on his feet. "I don't know about that, miss, I'm sure. The senator wouldn't want you to be..."

He gestured, trying to convey what he didn't want to say in words.

Which was that Hanno wouldn't want Sara to be the subject of gossip, to become the butt of the town, to be spoken of as an adventuress. Sara could imagine the murmured conversations over the sweet wine and cakes, even here, as she stood on the rolling deck, the wind in her hair:

Weeks among the rough sailors, my dear, unchaperoned, on her own. Whatever did they get up to on the rolling deep, I wonder? And from what I hear, she insisted on sailing to Alexandria, the wickedest place in the world! Good heavens, whatever next? Well, you know, I always said she wasn't any better than she ought to be. She always had a wild streak... and I'll tell you what else...

Gods, there had been a time when she actually thought such things mattered! But the captain thought they still did. How was she to change his mind?

Feet on the steps, making more noise than was strictly necessary. Sara turned her head. Jerem had come up from the main deck, a wooden bowl in his hands. He met her gaze, and he lifted the bowl slightly. "Captain, I brought your breakfast," he said. His face was as wooden as the bowl. His eyes hadn't left hers. "And I'll get you yours, miss. I hadn't heard that you was up yet. You ain't eaten since the day before yesterday. The senator said..." He broke off.

Sara watched him. There was something in his voice. He was telling her something, trying to send a message. And here was Marcus, strolling up the steps with his thumbs in his belt. She flicked an eye at him, faintly astonished, then back at Jerem. He half shrugged, in a rueful sort of way. "We didn't tie him up again, miss, afterward. It just didn't seem worth the trouble. The senator said we should loose him, and the senator was right. He was always right. Down to the very last words he said, miss."

The very last... What was Jerem telling her?

Father had said, "Now." She knew what he had meant, and so had Jerem. But just before that, he had said...

"It was a horrible time," she whispered. Her voice seemed distant to her, detached from her mind, and yet, and yet... "It's difficult to remember. But he said to trust Marcus."

"That he did, miss. That's what he said, all right. I heard him say it myself." Jerem was looking at the captain, now. "His very words, miss. His dying wish, like."

She blinked. Marcus stood there, still watching her, face set in the lines of a judge. He had said nothing. She stared at him, looking for some clue, and saw nothing. But Father had said to trust him. She wet her lips and switched to Greek. "Marcus, the captain thinks we should return to Carthage immediately. What is your opinion?"

His eyebrows rose a little. He pursed his lips before he spoke: "Hmm. Well, I know that the cargo includes sword blades. I saw them being loaded, after all. And I know the orders concerning ships running arms into Carthage. Ship and cargo were to be confiscated. The crew were to be condemned. Enslaved if they showed no resistance. Executed if they did. Captains were to be crucified to a floating cross and cast adrift." His emotionless green eyes had swung to the face of Obala. "I doubt that those orders have been changed. The war may be over, but Rome will never countenance Carthaginian rearmament." He shrugged. "As to the... mercantile aspects of the voyage, I have no opinion at all, naturally.

But it seems to me, on purely military grounds, that putting into Carthage with this cargo would be...unsound tactics."

The captain stared at him, parsing through the Greek. The recital had been a straightforward statement of fact, delivered in a judicial monotone. Obala's mouth opened a little, and it seemed to take him several attempts before he spoke. When it came, his voice was rusty, and his Greek sounded unpolished and crude, after Marcus's rolling periods. "What d'you think we should do, then?" he asked.

"Well, let me think. Not sail to Carthage. But the naval blockade will hardly be so strictly enforced now. Ships on passage are far less likely to be stopped and examined, unlike those actually entering the harbor at Carthage." Marcus seemed to ponder, bowing his head. Then he straightened again. "Yes, on balance, I would say that Alexandria is the best option for you. And as for me, I can easily send a letter from there, advising my father of my survival, and, who knows, perhaps negotiate a ransom. I believe that Master Harcar's decision was right."

Obala gave a jerky nod. The mention of Hanno's name was enough; it had turned the scale. He cast a glance astern, to where the last fleck of land showed above the waves, then looked at the shadows. "Come a point downwind," he called to the steersman. "Braces! Meet her. Thus. Very well thus." He drew himself up. His hands went behind his back. "All right. Alexandria it is," he said.

Sara was still watching Marcus. His face remained calmly judicial, severe, remote. His eyes turned to meet hers, but his expression didn't change.

"Thank you for your advice," she said.

He gave a formal nod. "It was nothing. Of course you realize that I spoke only of the military situation. I have no idea at all about what profit there might be in the voyage."

She might almost have smiled, he seemed so eager to assure her on that point. "Of course. It was the military situation on which I asked your advice. After all, what do I know of war or politics?"

"No doubt no more than I know of commerce."

"No doubt."

The ship had settled on her new course, with a strong following wind to lend her speed. She burst through the back of the next wave with a brilliant flash of spray that made rainbows against the rising eastern sun. Sara felt the shock of cold on her face and the salt on her lips, sharp and prickling. She was alive. And she was free.

CHAPTER 12

They saw only three sails on the run east. Two of them turned away and hurried over the horizon as soon as they saw *Heron*. The other tried to close, but *Heron* was to windward and easily able to work farther away upwind. By the time night fell, with heavier weather coming, they had run the stranger's masthead under the edge of the world.

Sara caught Marcus staring after it, looking moody. "I'm sorry," she said. "But that looked a little like a tremiolia. If we'd tried to hail her, she might have wanted to examine us."

He shrugged faintly. "Naturally, you couldn't risk that. I quite understand." His voice sounded forlorn.

She hesitated, waited, then made up her mind. "I believe I owe you a debt." She wondered if she should add that if it were not for him, she might not have been able to overcome the captain's ideas about what was proper.

He turned his head to regard her, his eyebrows lifting. "Not at all. To the contrary, in fact. I still owe you my life."

He cleared his throat. "I only regret that I have no means of paying myself. It's up to my father, you see. I am entirely in his hands."

And under his thumb, thought Sara, and you don't like it. "You did say that the Roman Senate would insist on the release of prisoners without ransom."

"I also later said that I would not try to escape, or go at all until I was ransomed—and I swore it by my lares and penates. It would hardly accord with my oath to hold myself absolved of it by order of the Roman Senate. Not even the Senate can dictate the value of my own oath."

"But surely I can absolve you of it. You swore the oath to my father, and his rights and chattels have descended to me. There are...there are now no other offspring."

She almost choked on the last words, and he heard it. He searched her face but made no movement. It was just as well, she thought. If he acknowledged it, asked about it, tried to console her, it would only make it worse. She watched his eyes narrowing and tried to read the thoughts going on behind them. He was doing the same with hers, she knew.

"Only I can deem myself quit of an obligation," he said at last. "I am the only judge of my oaths." His eyes lifted to the sea, to the curve of the taut sail, to the supple, living lines of the ship. He breathed in deeply, pulling the brisk salt air to the bottom of his lungs. "And if I choose to judge them severely, so that I can go on doing this a while longer, rather than go back home and work on the farm under my brother Primus, well, that's just my Roman stubbornness and stiff-necked pride, isn't it?" He turned back to regard her with owl-like solemnity.

She found herself returning the stare. She heard her father's voice again, his living voice, not his dying words. "My father told me that the Romans had fourteen words for 'stubborn,' and none of them were adequate," she said, almost to herself.

"Ah." Marcus nodded judiciously. "No disrespect meant, but I think he might have been wrong about that. There are in fact at least sixteen. My father calls me fifteen of them, and I use the sixteenth of him. But it's true, none of them are in the least adequate." He was still watching her face. She almost smiled, and then, to her own utter horror, she burst into tears. She turned to flee into the cabin, but that meant descending the steps to the main deck. As she came to the top of them, she found herself looking down at Jerem. He had risen to his feet, his hand was at his belt, and he was looking up at Marcus with murder in his eye.

She had to explain, even through the racking pain. "No, no, Jerem. No, it's nothing. He didn't say anything to upset me. It's not his fault. It's just me. I'll be all right, I promise. Look." She dried her face with her sleeve. "I'm sorry."

Jerem said nothing. He simply nodded and stood back to allow her to pass. But now it wasn't necessary to hide in the cabin. The very act of understanding what he was thinking and explaining herself to him had helped, somehow. Saying that she was all right had made it necessary to act as though it were true. She could straighten her shoulders, raise her head, and watch *Heron*'s sharp bow digging into the waves, catching them, shouldering them aside, racing on.

She watched the flight of the gulls and felt the lift and surge of the sea, its jewel colors gleaming under a clean-washed sky. Perhaps she could go on doing this, too, like Marcus.

Alexandria wasn't much interested in her feelings, anyway. The great port city at the western mouth of the Nile wasn't much interested in anything but tonnages and ladings, goods and profit.

The outer harbor was crowded, as always. Smaller vessels like *Heron* might wait days for a berth at one of the inner harbor's docks. Shore boats and lighters worked among the ships at anchor, selling everything under the sun, and many other things that were more usually trafficked by night.

Obala provided a rough tally of the cargo to the harbor authority clerk on the port galley. That urbane young man's eyebrows might have risen fractionally, but he nodded, made marks on his sheet, directed them to an anchorage, and took a fee, for which he produced a receipt. He hinted that an unloading berth would be available more quickly if a further, personal, fee was paid. Sara had been half-expecting that, and she watched while Obala passed over the three silver coins that they had agreed on. The official paused, sniffed, agreed that something might be ready by the following day, and departed.

Sara watched him go. She was wearing the best clothes she had. Her tastes had always tended to the plain, but the cloth was good. She had bound her hair back and tied it up with a single dark ribbon, but the ribbon was silk.

"I have some calls to make," she told Obala. "Jerem, would you escort me?" And in Greek, "Marcus Licinius, perhaps you would care to stretch your legs ashore?"

"You'll be calling on friends, miss?" asked Obala dubiously.

"By no means," said Sara. "Later, perhaps. First I must shop for some jewelry."

There was still some enjoyment in astonishing them, she thought, as she descended to the shore boat that would take them in. Watching their eyes open wide and blank surprise come over their faces. She asked the boatman for the set of steps nearest to the jewelers' street, and she allowed Jerem to pay him without another word. Of course, it would never do for a lady to be carrying money. Officially.

Her body had forgotten the land already. The steps seemed to move beneath her feet, and the little square at the top felt as though it rolled. But once she reached it, the half-remembered bustle and traffic assailed her nose and her ears. She could scent burning charcoal and hear the tap-tap of little hammers. The silversmiths were this way, down this street.

In the other direction, rather as she had thought, other metalworkers plied their trades. It had been the same in Carthage. They tended to need one another's products, so their shops were found in the same districts.

She paused. "Marcus Licinius, obviously you will be bored by this. Perhaps you might be more interested in the goods offered there." She nodded toward the larger of the two streets leading off. A specialized trade was in occupation here—swordsmiths who worked on finishing and burnishing blades. Close by, a scabbard maker stretched hides in the sun. Marcus shrugged slightly, but she smiled. "I won't be more than half an hour or so. Shall we meet back here then? Jerem will be quite enough escort for me, I'm sure."

A lady buying one or two good pieces was always welcome in the street of the silversmiths, even though the pieces might be small. And this lady was quite sure about what she wanted. A necklace of linked silver disks set with moonstones, to match earrings she already had. She was definite about the size and weight, and she wanted to price the set stones separately. She was shocked at the prices, though.

"What can we do, mistress?" asked one of the craftsmen she consulted. "Silver is scarce and dear. The price has doubled in a month—and it was high before, what with the war in the west and the loss of trade. But I can copy these in plate, and if you keep it polished, nobody will ever know..."

The lady said she had to consult her father.

Sara took her time. Already she was regretting the bribe she'd paid in silver coin to the harbor official. It was clear that she might have gotten away with less—she *thought* the man had looked too pleased. At last she turned and retraced her steps, making calculations in her head. Margins, commissions, how much markup, how many middlemen. She was surprised at the figure she eventually arrived at.

Here was the square by the harbor, and here was Marcus, arms folded, leaning on a wall, watching the traffic pass, and looking moody. He spotted their approach and shrugged himself upright. "Finished?" he asked, looking her up and down. Then he frowned. "You...didn't buy anything, then?"

"Everything was rather expensive," she replied. "But you? Did you see anything you liked?"

He flipped a hand. "The usual stuff. It's all right, I suppose. There's three or four good bladesmiths, and one of them was chatty. He was telling me that he's getting his steel from Syria now. Doesn't think much of it, but..." He shrugged.

"It's not as good as the Spanish metal, then."

"No." Marcus was beginning to frown. "Everybody knows Spanish steel is the best."

She nodded and turned. "Jerem. I think if you are to escort me around the town, you should be wearing a proper blade. Suppose you go and find out how much a plain sword is. You can say 'how much' in Greek, I think."

"S'all right, miss, I've got my..."

"It'll be a sort of badge of office. Go on, now. Marcus Licinius will protect me." She turned back, and spoke in Greek. "I've just told Jerem to buy a sword, since he is to escort me."

Marcus was staring her in the eyes. "I'm not at all sure that you need looking after. You seem to be managing perfectly well," he remarked slowly.

She smiled conventionally, as if he had meant it as a compliment. "By no means. I was hoping to arrive on the Maimonii's doorstep looking a little more prosperous. But at least having an armed retainer will help somewhat."

Marcus wasn't letting his face show anything. "No doubt."

"Would you care to come, too? The Maimonii will be flattered by the presence of a Roman patrician in their countinghouse."

"And perhaps they'll lower their prices. Or raise their offer for your cargo. Or do whatever you're aiming to have them do. No, thank you. I would ask what you're up to, but I think the answer would involve trade and commerce, so I won't."

She inclined her head and didn't pursue the point.

Jerem returned with a list of prices. Sara listened carefully, authorized a modest purchase, and waited again until he came back with it.

"They threw in a sheath, miss. I can work out a way to hang it. I've still got my knives, too."

"Show the sword to the Roman." And in Greek: "What do you think of this?" Marcus hesitated, his frown deepening. She sighed. "Oh, come now. No harm in giving me your opinion of a sword. Nothing could be more military than that, surely?"

He snorted, but he half drew the blade and held it slantwise to the light. Then he tested the edge, sighted along it, and flexed it. "Bit thick," he muttered. "Not a lot of spring. But it's workmanlike enough. Shallow fuller, and the hammer welding is competent—only one band along the edge, though." He slid it back. "I've seen far worse. Most legionary swords were like this until a few years ago, when we started getting Spanish blades. My father says..." He broke off.

"Your father says...?"

He shrugged, looking away, embarrassed. "It doesn't matter."

"It's all right, Marcus, I'm not going to burst into tears again." Nor was she. Sara was concentrating too hard on what he was saying.

He shrugged again. "My father says that it made a real difference. Spanish steel did, I mean. You could trust the blade not to break on a full-blooded stroke, and it could be made thin enough to thrust with."

"Really? A real difference. I see. And did you see any blades like that here?"

"Not Spanish ones, no." He looked away. "It seems that supplies have not been reaching Alexandria lately." On this, he bit his lip. Clearly it was more than he had meant to say.

"Ah." Sara was still staring at him, but her attention was inward. After a moment: "Well, that seems to finish our business here. I believe I'll hire a chair to make my further calls. Perhaps, Marcus, since you do not care to come with me, you might return to the ship."

He nodded, as if she had confirmed an impression he had, but his reply was coolly formal: "Of course. I do hope my advice was helpful."

"Yes, indeed. I hope you don't mind my consulting you on purely military matters like this."

"Not at all. Farewell for now." He turned his back and marched away toward the harbor.

She shook her head and groped in her purse. "Jerem, run after him and give him this for the boat fare. I'll wait here." She almost smiled, but of course that would only have annoyed Marcus more, if he saw it. It would confirm his impression that he was being manipulated. In that, of course, Marcus was right.

The Maimonii apparently had sources of their own within the harbor administration. Sara wondered how much the official had made from selling his information about *Heron*'s cargo. However, they were expecting Obala, of course. She had to address herself at first to an Egyptian clerk, who seemed to think that she had called to buy spices for her own kitchen, and who attempted to direct her to the shop. She had, of course, already priced the spices there.

But in time the Egyptian called a Greek agent who had heard the name of Harcar of Carthage, and he called Shimon Maimones himself. After that, matters moved swiftly. Within a few moments, Sara was seated in the private office. Jerem stood by the door, for the sake of propriety.

"My man does not speak Greek," said Sara, with a significant glance at him. Actually, she was sure that Jerem had some words by now, and it would be necessary for him to learn more if this was to become the normal pattern, but it would reassure the Maimonii.

Shimon called for wine and dismissed his servant. He poured with his own hands, watering it well from a stoneware jug, beaded with water, cold from a deep well. He sat back, cradling the cup in both hands.

"Your honored father, he is well?" he asked, his voice neutral.

Much could be said in a few words. He knew about the fall of Carthage, of course. He was actually asking if Sara bih-Hanno had come to Alexandria as a pauper, a refugee. He might have been acknowledging that Hanno Harcar's daughter had a claim of some sort on his charity.

Sara made her response directly. "My father is dead, alas. He died on passage from Lepida, eight days ago." She drew the fold of her mantle over her head, to show respect. But she could do that and still watch his face.

Shimon took his right hand off the cup and struck himself softly on the chest. "Ayy. Adonai watch over him. He was a just man and upright." And yet his voice showed no particular surprise.

"He spoke always with respect of the honesty of your house."

"We traded for many years, fairly and with profit to both. I am deeply saddened by his loss. Please accept my condolences. I will do everything I can to help his daughter."

She inclined her head and sat in silence for a moment. Then: "It is my hope that this happy relationship will continue...."

Of course it took some time, and for most of that time the conversation appeared to be simply the normal currency of polite talk. She need not have been so careful, as it turned out. He didn't try to cheat her, and the prices he offered were honest. Father had been right. But of course business was business, and Shimon was entitled to a profit, as he and Hanno had both said. You had to pay what things actually cost, and that cut both ways.

He noted down her requirements, drew a line under the totals, and nodded. "So much for the metals. The wool and the other goods I do not handle directly, but I can certainly bring a partner in, and it would not be right to charge a commission on that. The spices you wish to take in trade I have on hand. Etion will have the silks. Now, as to the precious stones...Indian gems, I believe you said. You do realise that these are normally sold in settings, rather than loose?"

"Not to the trade, I believe. I will be selling to the trade."

"Ah." He stared at her for a moment, but she said no more. "Well, I believe it can be arranged. The last monsoon's cargoes are still trickling in. Yes. Leave that with me."

"We will be docking, probably tomorrow. I'm not sure where they will put us."

"Ah." Shimon rose and went to the door. He beckoned, and a clerk hurried to take his instructions. He turned back again when he had finished giving them. "As to that, I think you can count on a berth at the Cyprus dock, just at the bottom of this street. After all, your cargo is in high demand, and a rapid unloading would be in everyone's interest. Shipwrights and chandlers are close at hand. I will put in a word for you at Shariot's." He paused. "I am intrigued, I must admit. One normally expects to *sell* unset gems in Alexandria, not buy them. Our craftsmen are said to be the finest, and we export the finished pieces."

Sara's eyebrows rose fractionally. "It's only a minor matter, and a notion of my own. Of gems, I am taking no more than would fit into a single case. But the finished-goods end of the jewelry market here is affected somewhat by the dearth of precious metals—silver from Spain, gold from Africa—and that is likely to remain so for some time, what with the situation in the west. You have the gems, but the settings for them are startlingly dear, and nobody is buying, at the moment. I have noticed a drop in the gem market, therefore."

Shimon cocked his head, curiosity in his eye. "That is so. I think myself gems would be a good investment until the price of metal stabilizes again. But you did not speak of an investment. You said you would be selling to the trade." He watched her, but again she said nothing. "Perhaps I can advise you. I give you my word on the Book that nothing you tell me will go beyond this room."

She eyed him warily, but this was a man she would have to trust, and his advice would be valuable. "Yes. I will be taking the gems and silk and spices to the best market for them, naturally. To where such luxuries will find ready buyers, their hands full of money that they're eager to spend. Where there is no shortage of looted precious metal to be worked into sumptuous jewelry, thus to assure them that they really are aristocrats and gentry." She paused and watched the comprehension dawn in his eyes, and his approving nod. It confirmed what she thought.

He breathed out, long and gently, through his nose. "The news of that enormous ransom arrived only last week. Speculation in silver and gold began immediately, of course. Prices have already soared, as you have seen. Your idea seems sound to me, then, though it needs to be executed quickly. The... distortion in the market will not last long." He walked around the corner of his desk and sat, arranging his robe. "Had you thought of taking on a partner?" he asked.

CHAPTER 13

The Maimonii were as good as their word. At daylight the following morning, *Heron* was towed to a prestigious berth in the inner harbor at the foot of Cutler Street and unloaded. The metals were removed under guard, sold for a price that Sara actually found it best not to think about, except as just a set of numbers. The rest was sold at the dockside by auction. Shimon Maimones had spread the word, and bidding was brisk. Sara spent the afternoon reckoning the profits.

She emerged from the cabin into the dusty gold of late sunlight and closed her wax tablet with a clap. "That's the last of it unloaded, I believe, Captain? All the stores and everything?"

"That's it, miss. She's as empty as a drum."

"Well. How did your discussion go with the yard?"

"The foreman told *me* he was busy, but then your—er—friend had a word with the owner. They'll have a slip ready first thing tomorrow. We'll haul her out and go over the hull. I don't think there's much wrong, but she could probably do with a scrape here and there, and a lick of paint..." He ran down. Sara caught the words "planking," "frames" and "caulking." She nodded as if she had understood.

"Good. I'll need your list once you've had a chance to see what needs doing. Now, the crew can be paid off here, if they would prefer, or..."

"Oh, they'll want to ship for the return voyage, miss. Perhaps they should get something on account, for a run ashore."

"I see. Yes, of course." She started to tap the tablet in her hand against the other palm and stopped herself. It would look nervous. "But I would like to ask your opinion. I thought it might be better not to make the return voyage immediately, while everything at home is in such turmoil. Of course, it's up to the crew whether they wish to sign on again or make their own way back. I'm sure there are ships bound for Carthage where they can find a berth, but I was wondering if I should look to sail elsewhere, for now."

Obala was frowning, and there was alarm in his face. Then he shook his head. "Miss, with respect...but I don't think so."

Was he giving advice, or telling her what he had decided? Would he try to exert authority over her? It all depended on that. She must not allow the idea to form in his mind. "Ah. I'm sorry to hear that, Captain. My father told me...but what would you advise?" She left unsaid what, if anything, Hanno had told her, but she knew that invoking his name would have its effect.

She watched Obala very carefully. It had been important that she spring this on him suddenly like this. He had simply assumed, and hadn't thought about it at all, of course. He must not have time to reflect now. But neither could he be allowed to think that she was giving him orders. He would balk at that.

He was groping for words now. "Why...I thought we'd return home. At once. Now that we're rid of..." Again he gestured, and as before, it was to say what he couldn't say in words.

She frowned, as though she were considering the idea. "I see. And what do you advise we should load for the return voyage?" Again she used the word "advise," a repetition that he hadn't noticed, but one that would limit him, even in his own mind.

He hadn't thought that far, of course. "Well, I don't know. Um...fine Egyptian linens, perhaps. Faience. Greek pottery...um. Grain, maybe? That's cheap in Egypt."

"Grain? *Heron* carry grain? Forgive me, Captain, but I didn't realize she was suitable for the grain trade." Sara spoke with transparent sincerity, sweeping a glance at the ship's fine lines and narrow entry. "But of course I am not to know such things."

Obala scratched his head and conceded the point. "Well, no, perhaps not grain. But other cargo..." He was floundering now. "Costlier goods. Murex. Um. Arabian incense. That sort of thing."

"Really?" Sara allowed her voice to become meditative. "I wonder how much money anyone has to buy such things in Carthage these days. The Roman army being in occupation, that is. The city is full of Roman soldiers, my friends tell me, and it appears that, well, things are a little difficult there." A meaningful glance up the hill toward Sara's friends, who had pulled strings to get Obala's beloved ship into dock faster, and who therefore knew things that he didn't. "Women being insulted in the street, and so on." Eyes downcast now, modestly on the deck. "And of course, the costlier the cargo, the greater the loss, if there are no buyers."

Obala tried to nod and shake his head, both at once. The various implications of what she had just said had undermined him, as she had intended. He hesitated. "Well, I don't know, I'm sure. But miss, your father wouldn't want you to...well...go traveling about the world forever."

I'm not sure that he wouldn't, actually. Why not? she asked inwardly. But that was the other Sara, the one who lived behind her eyes and was not allowed out. Openly, she only inclined her head in grave agreement, conceding before he had the chance to think further into it, or worse, put himself into her father's place. "No, of course not. But as a matter of fact, Captain, I had already taken your advice as to the cargo."

"My advice?" Now he sounded simply bewildered.

"Yes. I remembered what you said about *Heron* being no bulk carrier. It's in the warehouse now, already paid for, to be delivered on call. Costly goods, as you said. Silk, spices, gems. I'll look into your suggestion of Arabian incense, too." She opened the wax tablet, took out the stylus, and made a careful note. "It hadn't occurred to me. Thank you. It's good advice."

"Silk? Spices?" He was frowning deeply now. "Well, yes, Alexandria is the place to buy them, all right...."

"So I thought, too. I'm glad to have your approval,

Captain. But the question is, where should we take them? A rich cargo indeed. Luxuries, you might say. We need a destination where people have plenty of money to buy them. And I remember my father remarking that you should buy at source and sell at distance. Aleppo, perhaps?" She looked into his face as if mildly perplexed, clearly seeking counsel.

He frowned. But he was actually thinking about the problem now, not simply consulting his set ideas of what was right. "Aleppo...no, I don't think so. Not with silk. It's about the same price there as here. Corinth, perhaps, or Ephesus, or Rhodes, maybe...and then we could load...let me see..."

She almost sighed in relief. He had hardly noticed that the question was now not whether they would return to Carthage immediately, but where else they might go. But she continued to watch him with respectful admiration while he considered the possibilities.

"...then there's Athens...mind you, the port at Piraeus is a little crowded these days. Delos for slaves, of course...but no, perhaps not. No place to put them..."

Here came Marcus, stumping up the gangplank, a little ahead of schedule. She hadn't quite been able to time this exactly, but she had known where he was going and what he was doing, and she knew that he would come straight back—it was a point of honor, and anyway he had no money.

She could not interrupt the captain, but she could look, distracted, over his shoulder. He, of course, turned to follow her glance, falling silent. Marcus was climbing to the afterdeck.

"Ah, Marcus Licinius." Sara had become the welcoming hostess, a proper role for a lady. "I hope you were successful?"

He nodded politely enough. "Yes. There's an Ostian agent buying grain in the ship forum, or whatever they call it here. He'll accept a letter, though he won't be leaving for a week at the earliest. At least he's an equestrian, so one may *hope* that he won't immediately break it open and read it. I'll go and write it now. Gods only know how I'll put this to my father." He glanced sidelong at her. "It'll take weeks to get back to Rome, anyway, on one of those grain barges. And I'm still not sure my father will pay. Swearing not to escape has a funny sort of sound to it."

She shook her head. He was plainly worried about it. "You've already told me about the stubbornness of Romans. So did my father, and I can well believe it. I've said already that I would release you from your oath, and you have declined." She sighed. "I wish I could find a way to satisfy your prickly sense of honor."

"Oh, I'm not going to be difficult about it. I've got to go home sooner or later, and I know that. I'll just have to accept your consent and count myself in your debt." He sounded gloomy, and she understood why. He would be returning with his situation unchanged and with no share of the booty won at Carthage. Worse, under something of a cloud, a request for ransom over his head, even a thought of dishonor. Perhaps even worse from his point of view, he might never have another opportunity to go to sea.

She shook her head, sympathizing. "I'm sure it won't be so bad. No doubt Rome will have a great deal to celebrate, and of course your family will be glad to welcome you home." Marcus, as expected, snorted in disbelief, so she was able to sound indignant on his behalf. "Of course they will. You fought with courage and skill, were first upon the enemy deck, and you never surrendered, only being captured when you fell unconscious from your wounds. And then there were the pirates, to which we could also bear witness. I wish I could tell your family myself." She paused. "The captain and I were just considering where we might take another cargo. I'm afraid I've bought rather a lot of costly luxuries." A helpless little gesture, indicative of female weakness for pretty things. "It's a pity we can't return you to Rome ourselves, considering that *Heron* would be far faster, but of course that would be impossible." There. She had done it. Now she could only wait.

She couldn't watch Obala's face. She could only hope that it wore the same look as Marcus's—immediate unthinking acceptance, followed by reexamination, puzzlement at first, then genuine consideration, then inspiration.

"Wait a moment. Wait. Rome, did you say?" Marcus was staring at her.

Sara frowned as though nonplussed. "Well, yes, but that's impossible. The war—"

"The war is over."

"Well, yes, but—"

"No Carthaginian ship may trade with Rome. That would never be allowed." Obala sounded not quite certain of that.

"Stuff and nonsense," said Marcus. "Of course it'll be allowed, so long as Romans control it. You forget, I was with the fleet. We sent prizes in all the time. Carthaginian ships by the score will be coming in with returning soldiers and, well, booty and ransoms... no offense. It's only a matter of having the proper license...." His eyes were darting, his whole face animated. "The shipowners would be clients of Romans, in that case." He looked up. "Of course, of course. I should have thought of it before. If you become our clients—officially only, and for the nonce—I'm sure it will pass. The local resident in Alexandria can furnish a letter—he's one of the Hortensii, and our families go back—and then there's my father. He'll be a lot happier to see me if I bring back some renown, at least. And some suitably grateful Carthaginian clients, too. With a shipload of costly goods."

"But wait, wait." Sara was clearly astonished. "The goods... we can't... they're everything we own..."

"Of course. And they remain yours, in Roman law. What do you take me for? Some sort of thief?" He looked down his arched nose at them. "And, of course, my family has no interest at all in what you *trade* them for." A pause while Sara looked properly chastened. "But you do us a favor—saving my life and returning me—so we do you one in return—patronage. A trading license. As our clients, your success reflects well on us. In return, you show proper respect and loyalty. That's how it works."

Sara shot a glance at Obala now. He was shaking his head. "It still sounds like we'd end up owing your family a cut of the profits," he said, but there was speculation in his voice.

Marcus looked as though he'd found a worm in an apple. No, half a worm. "No. Not on any of your own goods. We are no robbers, we Licinii. It's inconceivable—and anyway if the censors found that we'd stolen profits in trade from a client, they'd...no, it's ridiculous." He looked away. "Of course, if later my father chose to make a business investment..."

Obala looked skeptical. "I thought you patricians couldn't engage in trade."

Marcus made an impatient gesture. "Gods above, man, what do you think agents are for? But at arm's length. It's a standard arrangement." He gestured. "*You* are the ones who trade, not us. If you ever need a loan, the first place you go is your patron, naturally. Strictly business for you, and an exchange of favors, perfectly proper between client and patron, for us. But even that's well in the future." He switched his regard to Sara. She watched him, inwardly amused, as he set himself to convince her. "At the moment, all I am proposing is that you sail to Rome with your cargo, and return me home so that I can present you to my father and gain some credit with him. That's all."

Sara looked at Obala, plainly asking his opinion. He pulled his chin, looking shrewd. "So, basically, we forget the ransom and get your family's support instead?"

Marcus grimaced. Putting it in such sordid terms discomfited him, clearly. "If you like."

"And you know people, too. Rich Romans who might want to buy silks and gems and such." Obala held up a hand as Marcus began to protest. "No, no, you wouldn't go around drumming up trade for us. Perish the thought, gods, no. 'Course not. But any patron can give a client a letter of introduction, can't he? That's only polite, ain't it?" Marcus subsided, thought about it, and gave a short nod. Obala frowned consideringly. Then he turned to Sara. "On the whole, miss, I think it might be worth thinking about."

"Do you really?" Sara stared down at the deck meekly. "I must confess, the thought had never occurred to me." It went unnoticed, except by the other Sara. She thought it was cheap and showy even as it was uttered, and she disapproved.

CHAPTER 14

The ship was hauled out of the water on a slip, and Obala went over her hull with a handspike, probing for rot. Before the sun was fairly up, he was rubbing his hands.

"Two planks to replace. That's all, only two. They're doing that now, on the nod. And there's a day's pay for five scrapers, and the riggers. We'll be ready to sail tomorrow, as soon as we've loaded. Quickest turnaround I've ever had in Alexandria." Obala sounded exultant. "And that cargo won't take long to load. I'll have to ship more ballast..."

Sara could allow him to describe the technical details to himself. It wasn't necessary to listen. She had paid half-wages on account to the crew, surprised to find that they all wished to sign on again.

"You're good luck, miss," one of them had said to her. She had smiled and let it pass.

The yard outdid even its own undertakings, and the ship was refloated before the tenth hour. Ballast and then the cargo was brought on board, the Maimonii providing armed guards to carry it to the dock.

"It's stowed," said Obala, climbing out of the hatch. He eased his back, blinking in the late light after the dimness of the hold. "We can sail at dawn." He shook his head and stared up at the masthead, where riggers were working on a new yard. "The faster the better, before the word spreads. And we strike straight across, sinking the land all the way until Crete, getting as far north as we can before the wind turns. That's why I'm rerigging her with a lateen, to lie up closer—." He broke off, and nodded toward the dock. "Here's your friend. And the Roman."

They were coming from the same direction, in fact, Marcus on foot, Shimon Maimones in a chair. Marcus simply marched up the gangplank, ignoring everything going on around him. "Well, it's done," he said when he reached the deck. "I have the document. No problem. That'll allow us to dock in Ostia, and I believe my father will do the rest."

"Thank you," said Sara. "That's very good of you. Ah, and Master Maimones. We also owe you a debt of gratitude. I really have no idea how I would have managed the shipyard without you."

Shimon Maimones took the hint, as she had expected. He simply bowed faintly. "Always a privilege to assist so respected a family. I have here a letter of my own, for my agent in Rome, with a request to extend his good offices also." He looked around him. "You seem to be on the wing."

"The captain says we may leave tomorrow morning. May I introduce..."

Shimon Maimones declined wine, claiming press of business, and made his farewells, having cast a sharp eye over the cargo, and exchanged a nod with the guard at the foot of the gangplank. Sara turned to the captain. "The crew?" she asked.

"They'll rejoin before dawn, or we sail without them. *Heron* only really needs four hands plus me, if we don't have to pull."

"You should take some time ashore, too, Captain. No doubt you have friends here."

"Ah...not exactly, miss, no. I could almost say the same to you. You've only been off the ship the once since you boarded." Sara smiled automatically, being careful to look down so as to display a becoming modesty. The captain was joking, of course. Bad enough being not properly chaperoned on the ship. Walking in the streets of Alexandria at night, escort or no escort—impossible!

"I'll say good night, then," she said.

She had bought fittings for the cabin, bedding, blankets, a desk that could be folded, a canvas chair. She'd even had a latticed door fitted, to replace the stained and shabby curtain. The place looked more like a room and less like a hutch. But her sleep was hardly better. Her brother and her father came to her again in her dreams. They said nothing, but they stared at her with sad and disapproving eyes, and again she awoke in tears, long before dawn.

"Crete. That's Mount Xiros, there," said Obala. He gave the faint line of serrations on the edge of the world a disapproving scrutiny. "No harbors this side, and bad holding ground.

Stand by to come about!" And to Sara: "Thank the gods it's blowing a nor'easter. Early in the season for it, but I'm not complaining so long as there's east in the wind. This'll carry us to the Sicilian Channel. Maybe through it, with luck."

Sara said nothing, wrapping her cloak more closely about herself. The wind had swung around in the night, and it was cold. The ship came around, bringing it on the starboard quarter. The sail was taken in and reset square to the mast. The distant coastline began to recede.

"Lucky again," growled Obala, looking at the steersman. The latter nodded, and they both made the sign that propitiates the wind god.

The god apparently appreciated the gesture, for he provided leading winds for the next three days, strong enough to kick the seas into a rolling, steep-sided chop. Obala grinned with satisfaction. "Just right," he said. "Not so strong that it's a danger, but strong enough that a galley won't be able to open her oar ports." He inspected the tumbling clouds and peered through the scud to where the coast of Sicily had just appeared to the west, gleaming in the rising sun. "Me, if I was a galley's skipper, I wouldn't be out in this anyway. So we'll turn now while we'll still have a point free if it backs west." He glanced at the sun and calculated. "Be through the Melita Reach before nightfall, maybe," he muttered. "Bear away a point."

It was as if his words had triggered the cry from the masthead: "Sail! A sail!"

"Sorry, Baal, I should know not to take you for granted by now." Obala raced down to the main deck and up the windward shrouds. He hung there like a bear in a tree, staring westwards, for a long minute, before descending.

"Edge down a little to him," he ordered. "Tremiolia," he offered, in response to questioning stares from Sara and Marcus. "Maybe he's a Roman."

Marcus pursed his lips. "Maybe he's not. The straits swarm with pirates. Segdians, mostly."

"If he's a pirate, we're to windward of him, and no tremiolia can stay with *Heron* on a reach in this."

But it was a Roman. Marcus identified the streamer at the masthead. "Appia Twelve. And see the row of winking reflections? Those are legionaries on his deck. No pirate would be as well-ordered."

Obala grunted. "Where's he off to, I wonder?"

"Home, most likely. Look—he's turning downwind."

"He's given up trying to beat east into this. Wise of him. He'll shelter under Dancer Cape until the wind moderates and comes around. Well, he couldn't catch us now if he tried. You're sure he's a Roman, though?"

Marcus looked impatient. "Yes, of course." He stared at the distant hull. "He'll use the Strait of Messina to get home."

"All very well for him. He's got oars for a short dash like that, even if the wind's against. We'll go around the west of Sicily. Even *Heron* could never run that narrow strait without a leading wind, and this isn't one. We might be windbound outside Syracuse for weeks if we tried it."

"He'll probably be home long before us, then."

It was said with yearning and yet with trepidation. Sara, listening, weighed the probabilities. If Marcus actually arrived in Rome ahead of them, he might act as a sort of advance agent, be able to make arrangements....

She shook her head in disgust at herself. If Marcus wanted to transfer to get home the sooner, he should be allowed to. Besides, it would prove that he hadn't been a prisoner....

Sara sighed inwardly. For the idea to be accepted, she would have to convince the captain and Marcus that it was their own. The proper line was to express sympathy for Marcus's wish to go home but regret that it was obviously impossible for him to transfer to the galley, for the seas were so *very* rough and high. The captain, his seamanship impugned, would then rise to the challenge.... It was all so manipulative. If only she could give orders like a man.

"You want to shift over to the Roman?" asked the captain of Marcus. He had asked it before Sara could speak, and she was surprised enough to close her eyes for a moment, thanking the gods for prompting him. Or perhaps it was Father's shade who had whispered in Obala's ear.

"I should rejoin the fleet at the first chance," said Marcus neutrally. "It would look odd otherwise."

"As if you was a prisoner, in fact," said Obala. "Yes, well. Can't have that." He ruminated a moment. "All right. We can follow him in and hail him, so long as you don't take too long. I don't want to waste a minute of this wind. But I think we should do it, miss."

Sara was still wondering what her proper response should be. Should she be regretful that Marcus was leaving, or should she ask for it to be explained to her, as if she hadn't understood? That would flatter them... but then there was the instant revolt of her conscience again. Slyness. Cajolery. Flattery. Deceit. How low would she stoop? Still…

It delayed her just long enough. Marcus turned to her. "You hesitate. I understand why." He glanced at Obala sidelong. "I wonder if I might have a private word with the lady, Captain? Of course you should watch to ensure there is no impropriety—but would you allow us a little space for a moment?"

Obala's eyes met Sara's. *Heaven alone knows what he thinks Marcus is up to*, she thought. She glanced again at Marcus and read his face. *But I can almost guarantee that it isn't what Obala thinks it is.*

Obala stepped back to the leeward side, and Marcus moved to the weather rail, away from the steersman, leaving at least a few paces between them. Sara followed him, conscious of a certain reluctance.

Marcus gauged his distance and dropped his voice. She had to lean forward to hear him, though she stood well within hand's touch.

"You don't need to worry," he murmured. "I realize it's only a…form of trade so far as you're concerned, but I gave my word. You are my family's clients, and I won't go back on it, even though I know you tricked me into it. I realized that as soon as I heard that Alexandrian merchant say that he knew you were going to Rome. You must have told him that a full day before I had the brainstorm you planted, but it makes no difference. I did give my word, and that's the end of it. So it won't matter if I get back to Rome first. It'll even be possible for me to prepare the ground for you, get a license issued, that sort of thing. You'll have an easier time of it…."

He went on, but she wasn't hearing. She struggled to control her reaction and failed. Without willing it, she broke in, "I didn't trick you! No. I . . . put a good idea in your mind, yes, all right. But it is a good idea. For both of us. You stop being a prisoner, even in your own mind, and I get, well, I get . . ."

"Yes, yes. Access to the Roman market. I understand. Everyone *profits*. No doubt it's a very good *trade*." The contempt in the last simply enraged her. He was dismissing her father's very words. She looked at his face, all haughty aristocrat, and suddenly the bonds she had wound around herself were breaking and falling away. It was freedom. Freedom to speak and not care what she said.

Contempt? She'd show him contempt. Her lip curled. "Better to trade than do what you do. There's blood on your hands, Roman. Glory? A joke! Tell me, what sort of glory was it to pilot my father to his death?"

"Eh?" His face showed only shock and consternation. It spurred her on.

"His last words. 'Even a merchant,' he said, echoing you. Even a merchant has honor. Well, so he has. More than you. You do what you do for a living. Slaughter's a *trade* for you." He gaped, and she rejoiced at it, and the words came as though the gods were speaking through her. "But he traded honestly, and when he fought and died, he died for the trade of honest men, and because you called him to it. Don't you dare . . . don't you *dare* insult his memory to me, speaking of trade in that way." Her eyes, hot and dry, held his for a long, hanging moment. She had not raised her voice. "Now go. Go. I trust you to do as you say. I know you'll keep your word, because of your pitiless honor. But remember this,

Marcus Licinius Corbo: I have kept my word, too, and better. When it comes right down to it, what have either of us to *trade*, but our good names?"

He stared at her. For a moment he remained aghast. Then a cold fury descended over his face. He drew himself up. He bowed slightly, stiffly. The captain was still watching them from the other side of the deck. Gods only knew what he thought they had been saying to each other.

Marcus spent a moment, clearly searching for a comeback, then rejecting the possibility as undignified. He bowed again, a stiff jerk of the head, and turned. He stalked over to the captain. "We are agreed, then," he stated loudly. "I should transfer to the Roman vessel. I can go in what I wear now. But my arms?" He looked around at Sara. "I am reluctant to leave them behind. I might need them. Another opportunity for *glory* might present itself."

She said nothing, turning her back on him.

They were opening a shallow road now, under the hook of a stubby, steep cape. Obala shrugged slightly and eyed the sheltered water in its lee. He rubbed a hand over his chin and turned his mind to the problem of transferring the Roman ship to ship, dismissing the quarrel. After all, it wouldn't matter if they were getting rid of the Roman. "We could manage some sort of sling once we're at anchor under Dancer. And if that Roman has a notion of what to do."

The master of the tremiolia *Huntress*, as it turned out, was a Rhodean, and he had a notion, but not quite the same notion as Obala. It took half an hour of shouted conversation once the ships were anchored within hail of each other, and another half an hour of passing a line and rigging a traveler to it. It bowed and came half-taut as the ships rolled, and timing was needed, but it worked. Marcus was hauled across with no more than a wetting, his armor following in a bundle.

"Thank the gods for that," remarked Obala. "We can get under way again."

Sara was watching the tremiolia's deck. Marcus did not wave. "Is he right, Captain?" she asked. "Will he really get back to Rome faster?"

Obala grimaced, unwilling to admit a deficiency, even by default, but he confirmed it: "That thing's got oars to get him around Sicily. Depends on how long this wind lasts. This is the third day of it. One more, maybe, before it comes west again. We've got to make all the westing we can before it does." The line, released from the Roman, was hauled in, dripping. He raised his voice. "Make sail!"

Sara heard the relief in his voice and felt it herself. They left the Roman ship to shelter in the lee of the point, and they headed out to the open sea again.

The wind didn't quite manage another day, in fact, and Obala watched, muttering, as it edged westward, dropping a little. He had to slant south, away from Sicily. Then, when he saw Africa through the murk of a rainy evening, he tacked, a touchy operation.

"Up as far as she'll lie," he said to the steersman. "Luff and touch her." And then, crooning under his breath, "Come on, sweeting, let's see how close you can come."

Heron answered him gallantly, it seemed. He watched the tip of Cape Bon for an hour before he reported himself satisfied. "We're almost holding our own on this tack. Morning and we'll see Sicily again, and then one more tack should do it."

Sara didn't entirely understand, but he seemed happy enough. She was content to leave the business of sailing to him. Obala would get the ship to Rome as fast as any man could. After that, it would be up to her again, and she hoped he understood that, if only by default, and wouldn't try to interfere. And it would be up to Marcus, if he hadn't forgotten all about them by that time.

Sara worried about that. It came between her and her sleep, and her sleep was poor, anyway. If she were wrong to trust Marcus, it might mean ruin. The Romans might simply confiscate ship and cargo for daring to enter their port. She could only plead to her own mind that it was in Marcus's own interest, and that of his family, to support her. Those calculations were done now. It only remained to find out whether they were correct or not. But her mind was tired of calculations of self-interest, of what would be profitable, of what shifts and subtleties would be necessary to bring it about, and it regarded the whole process with disapproval. And she was sorry for what she had said to Marcus. It had been true, but she shouldn't have...or perhaps she should. She didn't know.

She couldn't fully share, then, in the satisfaction when Obala reported that they hadn't lost too much in the tack, nor in the triumph when Cape Bon reappeared, this time to leeward, and the wind stayed true, just west of north. They could slant out well to the west along the African coast, then have the wind on their beam for the run into Ostia across the Tyrrhenian Sea.

"... and the great thing is, once we've weathered Sicily, the farther west the wind comes, the better!" Obala was almost grinning, spray gusting across the deck, Africa just visible through the scud. Already they were west of the Gulf of Carthage. The city lay downwind of them as *Heron* shouldered her way westward, winning distance across a northerly breeze. Obala eyed the clouds and the seas. "In fact, if the wind comes just one more point west, I'll put her on the port tack even now. And it will, sooner or later. Tonight, maybe."

Sara heard him and made the appropriate response, smiling, nodding. Another night. Nights were black and unfriendly. She looked to leeward, downwind. Home lay that way—Carthage, the city, the house where she had grown up, with her workroom that overlooked the harbor. But even if it still stood, the house would be echoing and empty, except for the memories.

More probably, it had been looted. Her loom was certainly broken into pieces, her mirror shattered, her small personal belongings flung to the winds. Or burned, the courtyard scorched, the fountain buried in ash, the room that had overlooked the harbor gone, fallen in ruin. She blinked tears back. She could not weep here as she could in the dark of the cabin. Then she shook her head, a quick twitch, impatient with herself. The mob, or the Romans, could not burn the land the house had stood on. Houses could be rebuilt.

But not by her. She was orphaned and had no close male kin. No woman could manage property. The city was supposed to appoint a guardian to do it for her. She could not choose who it would be. And, of course, he would immediately begin looking for the best offer of marriage for her. It would be like an auction.

Marriage. She had already amassed a fortune. It lay in the hold beneath her feet, and there was the ship and the land, as well. Certainly there would be men, even eligible men of good family, who would overlook her adventures for the sake of a dowry like that.

A dowry, certainly, but she would have to give it away to such a man, in return for the right to keep his household, to weave his cloth, to see his food prepared and served, to bear his children. To accept his protection. Father and Aram had not been able to protect her. Who would do it better than they? Sara stared at the sea and the sky, and her face was bleak. There was no protection. Only what she could make for herself.

She turned away and faced into the wind, and droplets of spray tingled on her cheeks and eyelids, prickling on her lips. She faced the cold, blustery wind that came from Europe. She faced north, toward Rome.

CHAPTER 15

"Well timed," said Obala. "To sight Italy in daylight. Always good to avoid running into the land in the dark."

He sounded relieved. The run from the African coast had been two days and three nights without sight of land, and he wasn't certain of his distance, though his direction seemed sure enough, from the stars. But there, purple against the ultramarine sea, were the peaks of the hills the captain had called the Tolfas, with flecks of islands far off, notching the northern horizon.

"We're a little to the north, but it's not a bad landfall at all." He looked at Sara sidelong. "Ostia by dark, likely. Don't expect too much, though."

So it proved. Sara was deeply disappointed in it. She was Carthaginian, a child of the mistress of the sea. Her city's focus and its lifeblood was its seaport, and it faced not toward the dun hills of Africa, but toward the moving, lively water.

Ostia, the port of Rome, was a dank huddle of thatch, brick, and wooden structures on the narrow, swampy flats of a river mouth. Wooden docks thrust out from muddy streets into turbid, filthy water just deep enough to berth a moderate vessel. Larger ships were unloaded in the open roads onto lighters, flat-bottomed boats that were then rowed or poled the twenty miles up a difficult river to Rome. Rome turned its back on the sea. Romans were farmers, herdsmen, peasant soldiers. Landsmen.

But the docks were crowded. Obala sucked his lips in when he saw it, and he swung about and studied the seaward sky. "Gods help us if a westerly gale blows up. The bottom's just mud. She'd drag her anchors for certain. And there we'd be, with nowhere to go but ashore in a heap."

There was no berth available, apparently. Boatmen came alongside, touting for trade, but they only shrugged when asked about one.

"They'll listen to money," said Obala, glancing at Sara.

"Do you think perhaps we ought to ask in the harbormaster's office if they've got such a thing? And the harbormaster might know where Marcus's ship has docked. What was its name again, Captain?"

She remembered the name very well. *Huntress,* a tremiolia with a Rhodean master and a detachment from Appia Twelve aboard. But if Obala was deferred to in small matters, he would be less inclined to bother about the larger ones. Or to notice that he was being managed. Sara observed her own thought process with mingled appreciation, disapproval, and actual shame. Obala deserved better of her.

But the harbormaster's office, while willing to find a berth in a day or two, had no record of the tremiolia *Huntress* or its passenger. "Hasn't been in," the clerk grunted, recording their own details in his log. He was apparently a Greek himself. He raised his eyebrows when he saw the letter from the Roman resident at Alexandria.

"You're Punic?" he asked. "From Carthage? Well, you can berth on the strength of this, but you can't unload until you have your trading license." He looked over a shoulder toward the inner office, where a balding, squat man sat at a desk staring out of the window, and then he leaned forward. "They don't like Punics here. The squeeze you'll have to pay will be quite some. What's your cargo, anyway?"

"Eastern goods," replied Sara. A girlish flutter of the fingers. "I hardly know myself. Perhaps our patrons will ease the matter for us. It'll be a couple of days before a berth's available, you say? Shame."

The clerk shrugged. He had already exacted the customary fees. It was nothing to him, clearly.

A day passed, with Obala scanning the morning sky for the redness that would foretell a storm. On the next day a berth finally became available. But there was no sign yet of *Huntress*.

"This is starting to smell, miss," said Jerem as they eased into the dock, a narrow jetty on rotting piles, for the use of which a large fee had to be paid.

Sara agreed, privately. She was beginning to worry. Nevertheless, appearances had to be maintained. She wrinkled her nose. "I agree. There's worse than dead cats in this water. Dreadful, isn't it?"

Jerem eyed her narrowly, then looked about. They were standing on the main deck forward of the mast, out of the way while Obala conned the ship in from his position by the steersman. Nobody would overhear quiet speech. "Miss, save that for Obala. He don't see much further into a plank than most. You know what I mean."

It took her by surprise, and Sara nodded sardonically at her discomfort. But there was no purpose to be served by unburdening. Except the unburdening itself, perhaps. "We have to wait; that's all," she said. "Possibly the ship put in at Syracuse, or Neapolis. Anything could have happened."

Anything could have happened. Her words came back to haunt her in the night. Without Marcus they had no standing. It all depended on him. She had been foolish to allow her plan to hang on a single element. Perhaps if she were to go to see his father herself...

But the journey to Rome proved fruitless. Senator Quintus Licinius Corbo was not to be found at his city residence. He had withdrawn to his country estate in Rietium, two days away in the hills. The porter couldn't say when he might return. He was in mourning for his youngest son. Nobody was being seen. Especially not Punics.

The door was shut in her face.

It was a change for her, this. To be seen as nothing, to be treated as if she were worthless. She returned to the river landing and let Jerem do the haggling over the return fare, standing quietly, worrying over money. Perhaps Marcus had turned up while she'd been away.

No. He hadn't. His ship was still not in. It was now the evening of the third day after their arrival, and there was no sign of him. Sara climbed the gangplank, frowning, biting her lip, with Jerem following.

Perhaps the letter to the Maimonii's agent would open

some doors. She reached the deck, considering how she might go on without help, and turned to Jerem. But Jerem was not there.

She halted. Jerem had not climbed the gangplank. He had been met at its foot by two men, one clean-shaven, the other bearded, both tall and stolid with blank, official faces. The clean-shaven one shoved a paper into Jerem's tunic, and the other touched him on the arm. *"Ereptor, ereptor,"* he said, enunciating clearly.

It was said, not shouted, but clearly, for all to hear, in a bored, official sort of voice, a drone, without emphasis.

Nevertheless, the effect on Jerem was instant and alarming. He twisted, threw the hand off, and there was a blur and a gleam and a movement, too fast to follow. The clean-shaven man was flat on his back on the splintery boards of the dock, with Jerem's foot on his chest. The other goggled down at the knife in Jerem's hand. Its point was at his throat.

The scene held, frozen. "You move; you die," snarled Jerem in Punic.

Sara was already running back down the gangplank. "Jerem. No." In Greek: "What is this?"

The man at whose throat the knife was poised moved only his eyes. They slid to Sara. "Tell him if he uses that knife, it's the cross for him. I'm the law."

Sara felt her heart sink. "Law? What law?"

The man swelled visibly. "The law of Rome. I accuse a thief. That's what I just called him. And we have papers for the captain and the owner of this ship. Them, too."

"Thief? What nonsense is this? We are no thieves." Well, in Jerem's case, not recently, anyway. . . .

The Roman shrugged. The knifepoint might have retreated a fraction. "Tell it to the judge. You'll get a fair trial." A tiny gesture. "It's all in the papers. I'm just doing my job."

"What now?" asked Obala, coming down from the upper deck. "What's all this?" To Jerem: "Put the knife down."

Jerem glanced at Sara. She nodded. He caused the blade to disappear and stepped back, reluctantly taking his foot off the other man's chest, allowing him to stand.

The man he had braced felt his neck where the knife had been, looked at his fingers, saw no blood. He looked up at Obala, who stood at the rail. "You the captain?" He backed away from Jerem and mounted the gangplank. He thrust papers at the captain, touched him on the arm, and said the same words as before: "Ereptor, ereptor," but this time in a sort of rapid, loud mutter.

"What's that mean?" demanded Obala.

"It's just a formality. The ship's under arrest. Read the warrant. You can't leave, is what it means. Cargo's under bond, too. That's until the matter's decided by the magistrate. Now, where's the owner?"

Obala flared up. "Matter? Magistrate? Who in blazes are you? Don't answer. It doesn't matter. Get off my deck, Baal fry you!"

The official's confidence had returned. No doubt this was more like the usual reaction. "Now, now, captain. No hard feelings. Just doing our jobs, and we'll go as soon as we're done. Don't try to leave, though. The port authority galley will have you before you clear the harbor. Now, where's the owner?" He consulted a paper in his hand, and his eyebrows rose. "Name of Hanno Harcar, a Punic merchant."

Obala shook his head. "What's it to you?" he began, but Sara stepped forward.

She climbed the gangplank once more, to face the official. "My father, Hanno Harcar, is dead," she said loudly and clearly. A small crowd of passersby was gathering on the dock to watch the fun. "He was killed by pirates on passage when we went to the assistance of a Roman ship. I am his daughter and only heir. Deliver your papers to me."

The man simply stared at her. "Dead?" He looked at the captain. "He really is dead?"

Obala glared but gave a short nod. "Hanno Harcar is dead," he said with heavy finality, and folded his arms. "We buried him at sea, three or four weeks ago. The lady told you the truth."

The official's eyes returned to Sara. "So you can give your papers to me," she told him. "I am Sara bih-Hanno."

He shook his head. "Sorry, miss. I couldn't do that. You're not named in the summons. I'll return the papers to the complainant. He can do what he wants about it."

"Who's the complainant? Who calls us thieves?"

"Look at the warrant. Tell your man to let us go." The official was eyeing Jerem with wary caution.

Sara nodded to Jerem, who stood back. The officials departed.

Obala was staring at the paper in his hand. "I can't read this. It's in the Roman language," he complained.

Sara took it and scanned it quickly. It made no sense to her, either. "Nor can I. We need an interpreter. . . . But . . . oh, no!" She stared, aghast. "Oh, gods. I don't need an interpreter for that." She pointed to one of the seals. "Look."

Obala looked, frowned, and remembered. He, too, had seen that seal before. "That Greek bastard," he whispered.

Sara closed her eyes and saw again the narrow little eyes and the bald head of the Greek merchant, Father's agent, in Tarbarca. She remembered how she had pleaded for his life. Marcus had said that she'd regret doing that. "Aratian. Yes. He's in Rome, too." She looked up at heaven. "Now we need more than an interpreter."

The gods listen, she thought later. Sometimes, anyway. And sometimes, they actually do something, though not often. But it was obvious that they had heard her then, and it must have tickled their fancy to act.

The captain had raised his eyes, too. But his gaze swept around the harbor, a habitual checking of the bearings of nearby ships. It traveled out, then past, then returned. His face went rigid. Sara followed his stare.

Across the river, at a far more prestigious wharf—it actually had stone piers—a ship was docking. Sara squinted and saw the uneven bank of oars, the broken rail, and the lighter patch on her deck. The ship looked lower in the water than she should be, too, and clear water was gushing in spurts out of a port at her stern. The mast was odd, as well....

"Do you see it?" asked Obala, and he was whispering, as if fearing to break an image. Sara shook her head. There was something...

"*Huntress*. It's *Huntress*." The captain's voice was wondering. "And she's been in a fight. Look. Fished yard, and the mast's been snapped off at the cap. Stone through the deck there, amidships. They've cobbled it over. And look. They've got a sail stretched over a hole on the other side, and they're pumping fit to bust. Must have started her frames." He paused and then went on, "But they've brought her in."

Sara fitted the details in over the last picture she had of that ship, with Marcus on her deck. She could hardly believe what she was seeing. But Obala was right. There was the image of the Greek hunt goddess with her bow and hound carved into the sternpost. It was the same ship.

She blinked, her thoughts whirling. She collected herself with an effort. "I must go over. If Marcus is…we need him…. Jerem. Come with me. Call a boat. That one will do, there. Hurry."

She gathered her mantle around her. Obala shot her one glance, saw her face, and raised his voice in a roar to the boatmen. She stepped down into the craft, Jerem followed, and they were rowed across the basin.

A ladder led up to the dock, but they were stopped at the top. A soldier in helmet and armor stepped in front of them, saying something. Jerem slid in between, his face impassive, his hand at his belt.

"No, Jerem. Calm." Sara faced the man. "Marcus Licinius Corbo," she said, enunciating clearly.

He shook his head and said something in the Roman language. She ignored it and said the name again. She pointed at *Heron*, across the basin. "My ship," she said. He looked, and she saw the flare of recognition in his eyes. He glanced over his shoulder and called a word.

Another soldier turned and approached. This one wore a helmet with a transverse crest and a feather. "Marcus Licinius Corbo," said Sara again.

The officer shook his head. "In ship," he grunted, in heavily accented Greek. "Hurt. Who you?"

"His client. Sara bih-Hanno." She used the Roman word, as Marcus had. "Jerem. Get my medicine case from the ship. Hurry." To the Roman: "I am a surgeon. Fixed his wound last time. Here." She pointed at the man's own thigh. "And here," pointing to his head. Soldiers compared scars.

He hesitated, then nodded. "Good work," he said. "All right. You come."

They had brought Marcus out on deck. She ran across the gangplank. There were others wounded. She scanned him briefly. He was as white as a sheet, insensible, his breathing labored, his wounds roughly bandaged.

She felt the aegis dropping over her, the cloak that every physician uses, covering her with calm authority. She took a deep breath and began the examination.

Some time later, Jerem was at her elbow again. By that time she had seen that most of the wounds were cuts that had been roughly bound up in the blood, and some of them were still weeping, but that the real problems were a broken left arm and a depressed bloody bruise over the right lower ribs, apparently made by a sling bullet. The bone would need setting. But the chest wound and the abdomen below it were swollen from internal bleeding. It was putting pressure on his lungs. And no doubt it had damaged the liver, which was somewhat enlarged—probably he had had marsh fever at some point.

She looked up. "These wounds are new. Two days, no more. He'd be dead if it were longer."

"A galley, off Naumatia. Bloody Segnians. We caught them boarding a coaster yesterday morning. Bastards. There were a lot of them. We had to limp in with the wind against, as it had been the whole way up from Sicily." The officer licked his lips. "We've no surgeon. We've sent for one, but there are no good ones here."

She shook her head. "The chest wound must be drained, and the bone set. It must be done now, at once."

They shrugged and shook their heads uncertainly. It wasn't permission, and it wasn't refusal. They didn't know what to do. "His father has the say. . . ." said the officer, temporizing.

"His father is three days' journey away. He'll be dead by then." They looked at each other, and she followed up. "I hope you're willing to explain to Quintus Licinius Corbo how it was that you stood there and let his son drown in his own blood." She pointed to Marcus's iron ring. "Better you than me. But you'd better send to him, quickly."

That did it. The officer blinked, considered, and then gave orders. They picked Marcus up in his hammock. Some of them went ahead, pushing people out of the way. A table outside a wineshop was cleared. Sara put down a silver coin. "A crock of the roughest, sharpest, sourest red wine you have. Now, please. And a scrubbing brush. Yes, a scrubbing brush. You've got a fire, I see. Boil these dressings." She poured the wine over the rough boards and scrubbed it off with lye from her bag. The proprietor said something, a discontented rumble. She threw him another silver piece and thereafter ignored him. "Lay the patient down here. Jerem, my bag." Again the wine, to cleanse the silver-bladed knife. "Hold him off that side."

She took the knife. Yes. There was the blood pool, just there, under the short ribs. She felt for the muscle layer, found it, laid the knife against the skin, and cut just past the fibers. Blood poured out in a shocking torrent.

"You kill him," said the officer, aghast.

"No. This blood was lost to him, anyway. Look at it. Dark, already clotting. If we left it there, it'd press his lungs up. See. Already he is breathing more freely. What's more, there's no froth in it. That's good. It isn't from the lung. Now we pull the rib up, to take the pressure off. . . ."

The flow was falling away to a trickle. Sara nodded. "Good. I'll let that drain completely, and I'll stitch it presently. Now the arm. Jerem, help me. It's like the last time you did this, on the other Roman soldier. And you, soldier, here. Pull. That's right. It's in place now. Hold it like this, cupping your hands under his armpit. Pull harder. That's it. Now hold it straight while I get the splints in place. Very good." One of the fingers was broken, too, and that had to be splinted as well. Then the stitching. The superficial cuts had clotted and were well enough, after cleaning, with a bandage, but there was a nasty gash on the sword arm that needed careful work. Then there were the other wounded.

The afternoon faded into dusk. The light failed. She stepped back at last. Fatigue swooped down like a striking hawk. She staggered and clutched at the edge of the table.

CHAPTER 16

Marcus hadn't regained consciousness. They'd spooned some soup into him, but he choked on anything but thin liquid. He had been carried back aboard *Heron,* where at least he could receive competent care in a ship that wasn't actually in a sinking condition.

He was breathing more freely, but he was a dead, stark white, his freckles standing out like flecks of paint. It was a race now, to see if he could make up the blood loss before wound fever developed, and after that it depended on how bad it was when the fever came.

His abdomen had been intact. Sara was sure of that, at least. And there was no deadly bubbling in the lungs. It was a matter of waiting; that was all.

Silence in the cabin. She sat holding Marcus's hand, feeling for the dead coldness that would mean gangrene starting. Obala broke it. "We need an advocate, then." He was continuing a conversation that he had started not long after they had brought Marcus aboard and had gotten him into the cot. Sara had actually forgotten about their other problems.

"Yes. I wonder how we're going to pay for one?" she asked, still distracted.

"The cargo is worth…"

"The cargo is in bond. We can't touch it." Sara was fearful, angry, and very, very tired. For once, she hadn't deferred and had actually snapped at him.

Another silence. It seemed to go on longer.

"So what are we going to do? The hearing is the day after tomorrow. I managed to get that much out of the street copyist I took these to."

"I don't know. I just don't know." She groaned and eased her back, already regretting her sharpness. It would do no good to have Obala resenting her as well. "I'll have to consult a Roman clerk. I can buy an hour of a scribe's time. But nothing is free."

An hour after dawn, Sara sat back from the writing tablet and massaged her eyes. She'd had nearly four hours' sleep. "I've reconstituted my father's accounts as close as I can, but it amounts to no more than what I say. Aratian will undoubtedly have well-attested books of his own." *Father, I have done my best. I hope it's enough.*

"It's only his word against yours. And what's it to the Romans? Why should they care?" Obala was still looking for breaches in the walls that enclosed them.

"That legal clerk charged me a thumping fee to tell me, among other things, that they have a formal treaty with Naxos, Aratian's native city, each to afford the other's citizens the protection of their laws. Of course no such consideration applies to us. We're Punics. And there is the cargo. Aratian's made the largest claims he could dream of, but even his dreams would only dent the value of that cargo. The Romans can levy any fine they want to on top. So for them it's easy money, and we have no standing." But he also said that Roman law made me the owner of ship and cargo, Sara thought. To do with as I wished. Not have to give it up to some man. And it remains mine, even if I marry.

"We're easily robbed, in other words." Obala broke into her thoughts.

Sara didn't answer. She glanced at the cot, where Marcus was twitching a little.

"Where will the court be held? In the Temple of Justice, or whatever they call it here?" Obala was leaning on the doorframe, filling it, with the door open to the breeze.

"No. It will be heard here, on the dock, by the port magistrate. Incidentally, as owner, I am myself counted as part of the assets that have been seized. And you have been charged with theft and have no means to make restitution. Jerem, too."

Sara looked up and saw that Obala's face had lost all expression. In effect, that meant being sold into slavery, if the court decided.

She shook her head and checked Marcus again. He was stirring, but there was some fever. She knew that was inevitable; she also knew it was his body striving to heal itself. But he began to babble in the night, and she sat with him, bathing him, trickling boiled water into his mouth via a rag twist, until Jerem took over for her, with her own body crying out for sleep.

The court arrived not long after dawn the following day.

The magistrate was in formal toga, with a dignified bearing and an oaken staff, and the proceedings were in Greek. Apparently most merchants were Greek-speakers. There was the usual invocation and reading of titles and documents. A pair of clerks, one Greek, the other a Roman in tunic and cloak, recorded. Bailiffs kept onlookers at a respectful distance. The court was held standing, on the rotting dock at the foot of the *Heron*'s gangplank.

Aratian was there, in person, with his advocate, who presented books and papers. The reading of the formal complaint took nearly half an hour. Kidnap, assault, threats of murder, robbery, fraud. Sara shrugged. Let them say what they liked. She was too weary to care.

The advocate was a sharp-nosed balding man, thin as a vulture, in a legal robe. Questions were pointed and unavoidable. Sara, as a mere woman, was not a witness, of course, so it was Obala who sweated to answer them.

"So you admit that you kidnapped and held my client to ransom?"

"No! We asked no ransom, and my master let him go without one, though Aratian had tried to rob him."

"I would call some three thousand drachmas' worth of ship's stores a substantial ransom. And let him go? No such thing! You attempted his murder by throwing him into the sea!"

"With a float, just off the point..."

"Lucky he could swim. Not so lucky for you, of course. So, your master was in a commercial dispute with my client, you say. Why did he not try his claims in the local court? Frightened of the verdict, was he?"

Obala simply looked bewildered. "What court? It was in the middle of a war. The Romans were a day's march away."

"Oh, of course. So it's all the fault of Rome! I might have known it." The advocate looked around with satisfaction, and the judge frowned. "All law and all justice were lost, and you could do whatever you liked. So you thought. But it wasn't lost, you see, for here you stand in a Roman court, to receive Roman justice under Roman law!"

Sara shut her eyes. It was going worse than she had feared. Obala looked like a bull bothered by a stinging fly, shaking his head, glowering, staring wildly about. He glanced at her in mute appeal. But she had no help to give him.

He protested, "No, no. I didn't mean that. Look, Aratian owed my master money, not the other way around...."

"My client has presented his accounts, signed and sealed, in order, dated and properly witnessed. What have you shown the court? A hasty scrawl, no more than notes you made up here and now. Lies. All lies. He owes you nothing. To the contrary."

"He's saying that he sold my master's cargoes for less than nothing! What sort of trade is that?"

"Oh, I see! The situation was total chaos, you say, no law, no court, no redress, so you could do whatever you liked— but my client was supposed to obtain full commercial value for those cargoes anyway, as if it were time of peace. Come, sir, if you're going to tell a pack of lies, at least make them consistent!"

"Those cargoes were worth much more. In Carthage..."

"This is not Carthage. Carthage is immaterial. What your master was in Carthage doesn't matter here." Carthage is not powerful anymore. We can ignore it. Sara closed her eyes. *Father, they dishonor you.*

Obala swelled. The comment had been meant to goad him, and it had succeeded. "He was being cheated by a shifty twister of a Greek liar, and..."

"Ah?" A silky smile. "My client is a Greek, certainly, though now a Roman client. Why does that make him a liar?" The advocate gestured toward Aratian, who took the cue, drawing himself up like nobility affronted.

"No, I didn't mean..."

"So you assaulted Aratian, the Greek, the client of Rome. Threatened him. Put knives to his back, and when he demurred, brutally robbed him of his seal and forged a document with it—"

"No, he sealed the bill himself. I didn't have to say anything to him."

"That's hardly to be wondered at, with your knife in him, is it?"

It went on. They finished with Obala at last, then began on Jerem. But he couldn't even speak Greek and simply stared. After some time, a Punic interpreter was found, but it made little difference. Jerem simply said nothing, admitted nothing, and denied everything, a dull, sullen, monosyllabic repetition. Sara knew it was useless. They wouldn't believe a word, and—she sighed—they had reason not to. At length they dismissed him.

Aratian was called. He told the court of his pitiful struggle in the hands of his captors, the captain's brutal glee, and the murderous violence of that thug from the Carthaginian gutters. Obala filled his lungs, and only Sara's quick clutch at his arm kept him silent. It wouldn't have helped.

She returned to the cabin. Marcus was stirring faintly, muttering in his fever dream. She got some more soup into him and sat with him for a while, returning for Aratian's questioning by Obala. All the captain could do was to tell him he was lying. Useless. The Greek was too well-coached. He simply did a good imitation of outrage at the suggestion, the very image of insulted propriety.

A long morning's work. All useless, all worse than useless. When the market value of the cargo was entered into the record, the Greek clerk couldn't stop himself from whistling, drawing a glance from the magistrate. Sara was astonished at it herself. She had been right to come to Rome. And, at the same time, horribly wrong, of course.

Aratian's advocate slid forward. "That is the case for the plaintiff, Justice. I think we have heard all the witnesses. You have seen all the documents, of course."

The magistrate nodded. "What amount of compensation was demanded? Clerk?"

"Twenty pounds of silver, plus damages in the value of fifty further pounds of silver, plus punitive damages of as much again. Plus costs of four pounds of silver. Total, two talents plus twenty-four pounds of silver."

"Hmm. Call it the eighth part of a talent of gold. Yes. But of course we must not allow a criminal actually to profit from his misdeeds. That would never be just. The rest of the cargo's value is...yes, I see. Well, no doubt a further fine could be levied, to the full value of the criminal's profit." The magistrate glanced up at the sun, which was approaching noon. "Are there any further witnesses?"

Sara nudged Obala. He spoke up. "Marcus Licinius Corbo, a Roman citizen, lies ill in the ship. He was there at the time. He would stand witness for us, if he were able."

The magistrate's eyebrows rose sharply. "You have a Roman citizen aboard your ship? Marcus *Licinius Corbo,* did you say?" He received Obala's nod and shifted to Aratian's lawyer. "You said nothing about this."

For the first time, the advocate blinked slightly. "I knew nothing of it, Justice." He turned his head to receive Aratian's wide-eyed stare and faint shake of the head. "Nor does my client." He bent his head to a quick whisper, asked a question in the same tone, and turned back to the judge. "My client says that no such person was present. But this...alleged witness is ill, is he? Unable to testify? How...very convenient for these people. An obvious ploy, in fact. Surely, Justice, you will not allow so transparent a fraud to interfere with the orderly dispatch of Roman law?"

He received a fishy stare from the judge. "It will hardly take much of the court's time to resolve the matter. If I am permitted to board the ship, I can see for myself." He glanced up at Sara, who stood at the ship's rail.

She blinked in surprise. "Permitted? How can I not permit you?"

The magistrate frowned impatiently. "The ship is your property," he intoned, his voice frosty. "Even a magistrate may not barge into private property, except to seize a malefactor in the course of his crime or flight. Force is not law. You are in Rome now, not some barbarian hovel on the edge of the desert. Do you grant permission?" He glared up at her, his face an iron mask. A Roman mask.

Sara glared for a moment, and in that moment saw much. She stepped aside. "Of course, Justice. You honor me."

The court removed to the cabin, crowding it out entirely, standing close-packed, heads bowed, under the deck. "I'm sorry for the crowding, Justice," said Sara. "He shouldn't be moved. It might open his wounds again."

"And this is Marcus Licinius Corbo?" asked the magistrate. He asked it of Obala, ignoring her.

"It is," said Obala.

The judge shook his head, for a moment becoming human. "I don't know him personally. His face is not unlike the senator's, whom I have seen at a distance." A hesitation. "He wears the iron ring."

Aratian's lawyer gestured impatiently. "It means nothing, Justice. This is an imposition on the..."

He was interrupted. Marcus spoke up suddenly. "Sing, goddess, of the wrath of Achilles, the son of Peleus..." he said, loud and clear, in a voice like a child's.

Sara shoved a clerk aside and felt Marcus's brow. "He is fevered, Justice. He should be bathed now."

The magistrate shook his head. Again he did not reply to her. "Well, he knows his Homer, anyway," he murmured. The recital went on under his words, dying down to a thready, whispery mutter as Sara began applying wet cloths, wringing them out in a bucket of cold water.

Aratian's advocate was swelling with outrage, or a good imitation of it. "Justice, this is a farce. Any actor may wear a costume. It's transparent nonsense. If this...person were truly a Roman citizen, let alone the son of a distinguished family, where is his retinue? Where are his clients...?"

"We are his clients," said Sara, ignoring her own official invisibility. "I am. So is the captain, so is Jerem, whom you accuse..."

She was simply ignored. The lawyer's trained voice rode over her, as if she had not spoken. "Where is his family, his kin? Come now, Justice! It's novel, no doubt, to introduce a witness who can only rave, but really, it will not do."

The judge's face had retreated into itself, becoming a pattern of iron grooves. He stared narrowly at the advocate, then down into the sweating face of Marcus. "A witness must be competent to be examined," he said, softly but clearly. "And the witness must speak for himself. He must be the one to state his name and condition. Another may not do it for him. And the court can only consider the evidence brought before it, not what someone says would be the evidence if it could be brought." It was a rapid mutter, the words of a man reminding himself of something known, something that was settled and plain, of long standing. The judge nodded to himself. He drew himself up, ignoring a sudden tumult on the dock outside, a babble of many raised voices. "Therefore, I find that this witness is not fit to give..."

The ship rocked. Footsteps sounded on the deck. Sara, looking up, saw a flicker of movement, white and scarlet, a gleam of metal. Aratian, standing by the doorframe, was thrust violently aside. Obala was shoved unceremoniously out of the way by a very large, knobbly man in a scarlet tunic, widely belted, with a cudgel swinging from the belt. Shouts could be heard, an uproar of voices. Jerem's hand went to his own belt, and Sara glared at him, grimacing, her hand making a cutting gesture. *No!*

The magistrate looked up in fury. "Who in Hades are you, and what do you mean intruding on a Roman court?" he roared, a sudden military bellow.

The large, knobbly man only stood aside, retreating out of the doorway. Another person took his place, a smaller man with the same eagle nose as Marcus, but gray of head and even narrower of face, his tunic and cloak of beautiful white wool, but covered in dust from the road. Harsh lines ran from the corners of his mouth to the jutting cheekbones, and an old straight scar crossed the brow from the left eyebrow almost to the hairline—Sara noted automatically that it had healed badly, stretched and puckered. Whoever had treated it had not known his business.

But her surgical observations were instantly driven from her head. The man spoke, pushing a hand forward in an emphatic gesture. Sara saw the dull gray ring, and she heard the name Marcus Licinius. She nodded and rose, standing beside the cot, and motioned the magistrate out of the way. A miracle. He moved.

"Here he is, Senator. Here is your son," she said.

CHAPTER 17

The Licinii advocate bowed to the magistrate. "That is the case for the accused, Justice. You have heard how the accused, although they were Carthaginians, cared for a Roman cast onto their decks, treating his wounds and faithfully nursing him back to health. You have heard witnesses who told you of how the accused came to the assistance of a Roman vessel assailed by pirates...."

Thanks to the Licinii resources, thought Sara. The senator's agents had found in Rome the under officer and three of the legionaries who had been in the Roman ship off Spain, and they had brought them to Ostia as fast as horses could carry them.

"...and you have heard how the Carthaginian maiden Sara, a skilled surgeon in her own right, healed the Romans after that engagement. You have heard from reputable Roman citizens that Marcus Licinius Corbo, a Roman, went voluntarily with them, because he knew they would return him to Rome the quicker, and that he was justified, for they faithfully put him on a vessel of the Roman fleet at the earliest opportunity, without ransom, and in no expectation of reward. You have heard how other Romans were healed, helped, and assisted by them. You have heard of their respectable connections and long history as a trading house, no matter if they be Punic—and after all, who is their accuser? A Greek, no more. And you have heard of how they again saved the life of Marcus Licinius, for though he still lies incapacitated, the shadow of death has passed from him, and it seems he will recover—thanks only to the skill of this lady."

The advocate paused. He was a tall, beautifully spoken man in a perfect white toga, full of the dignity and authority of the law, towering over Aratian's ratlike little squib like a lion over a jackal. "Above all, Justice, you have seen for yourself that they came to Rome voluntarily, submitting themselves to Roman law, in the expectation of fair treatment. I ask you, Justice, are these the acts of thieves? And against this long record of goodwill, of service—of faithful and even, yes, noble service to Rome—what has my friend to put? A mere accusation, falsified out of hand by the very documents he produces. Those so-called accounts are nonsensical, as distinguished witnesses from the Roman treasury itself and other excellent men of affairs—Roman citizens all—have attested before you, and to those expert opinions, my friend has nothing to say. Therefore, Justice, you must know that these . . . papers"—a contemptuous gesture—"are only lies in writing."

Sara sighed. Roman law seemed to go in for long, rolling speeches, even on the dockside, among the wheeling gulls. The Licinii advocate, it would appear, was only getting warmed up. She lifted her eyes to the background, looking out over the court, grouped by the gangplank, from the deck of the ship. This wasn't the splintery wooden wharf where they had first berthed. This was a stone-built dock, apparently the property of another Licinii client, and *Heron* and the court had been moved there. There was far more space, and yet the crowd of onlookers was much sparser. Apparently the Licinii guards at the landward end of the quay were keeping the mob out, whether the court was in theory public or not.

That allowed Senator Quintus Licinius Corbo space, obtained without undignified shoving. There he stood, in the same foursquare posture, his face unchanged. It hadn't altered a whit since he had barged into the cabin and taken charge, demanding a recess "so that a distraught father may greet his son, sore wounded in the service of Rome."

Distraught? He hid it well. He had started organizing immediately. People had flowed in, first an Alexandrian physician who had checked Marcus's injuries, stated that he could not have done better himself, and, until elbowed aside, was deeply interested in Sara's stitching technique and where she had learned it.

Then the advocate, and the petition for a grant of two days' grace to find other witnesses, the swift instructions to the senator's head of security, and all the rest, with Marcus still babbling and twitching in the cot. He was still lying there, but his fever was down now for longer each day. Now he slept, they were getting more food into him, and his color was better.

Sara watched the senator's face. He had listened to her, through an interpreter, and then he had questioned all the others, separately and alone. He had nodded when he heard the physician's report. He had looked her in the face, his eyes boring into hers. Then he had simply acted as though it were all ordained. His clients were falsely accused. They had been faithful to him. It was his duty to defend them.

The advocate had ended his summation. Sara noticed it only from the silence. The magistrate drew himself up. He struck his staff on the stones of the quay, once, twice, three times.

"Judgment," he said, and paused.

"I wasn't certain that I'd understood. They're actually going to throw Aratian off a cliff?" asked Sara.

The advocate was standing uncomfortably hunched under the low roof of the cabin. He checked with his patron, received his nod, and answered her. "That is the formal sentence. If he is within reach of the court in fourteen days, yes, he will be hurled from the Tarpeian Rock as a false accuser. But he has time to depart. He must go and never return."

"Good riddance." It was a croak. They all froze in place, struck silent.

All except Quintus Licinius Corbo. "Awake, are you?" he grunted. "And apparently in your right mind, as much as you ever are. It's about time."

"Thank you, Father. It's wonderful to see you, too," croaked Marcus. He shifted slightly in the cot and bit his lip, not allowing himself to groan.

His father's face hardly moved. Sara, hurrying to help, nevertheless saw the fleeting fear on it, before the older man enforced Roman steeliness on his features again.

"Hmph. Very clever. Always a smart reply." The senator cleared his throat. "They tell me you did well enough against two sets of pirates, although you also seem to have spent a lot of time flat on your back. Where you will be for some time yet, Mistress—um—Harcar tells me. It would appear that she knows what she's talking about, so you'll listen to her and do as she says."

Marcus had managed to shift slightly onto the other hip, his face carefully blank. Sara repacked pillows to support him. "Certainly, unless she instructs me to get up and perform a jig."

Silence. The senator shook his narrow head, then looked out of the doorframe, where late afternoon light slanted in. "I've made sure of that trading license," he said, apparently to the thin air. He glanced back at Sara's face. "Least I could do. And there's a couple of shipping agents I know who can probably use a fast vessel like this one. I'll have a word with them." He rose and stood looking down at his son. "Well, I'll go and put the plans for your funeral games on hold for now. I'll be back tomorrow. Mistress Harcar says you can probably be moved in a few days, so you can come home then. Your mother will be pleased." He looked away again. "So will I." It was said as though it was a shameful admission. But the senator nodded, turned his head, looked his son in the face, and said it again: "So will I. Farewell."

And he was gone without another word, his retinue following. Sara stared after him, shaking her head almost in chagrin.

"Yes," murmured Marcus, after a moment, watching her. "He is, isn't he?"

She stared out of the open doorway. "I think he is doing his best to tell you he is overjoyed, that he loves and has missed you and was in terrible fear that he had lost you. He is saying this by doing things for us, because he can't say it to you in words."

She heard his faint snort and shook her head again. "He also told you to listen to me, you know. And you said you would. Once more I find myself holding you to your word." She looked down at him. "And knowing that it will bind you. My father told me to trust you. And I know I can."

There was a long pause. Sara returned to gazing through the open doorframe. Beyond it, beyond the deck, she could see the water, with the setting sun glowing on it. It seemed like a long time before Marcus spoke again. "Ah. About that. I owe you an apology. I was unjust. I spoke without respect for the . . . profession of your father, an honorable man. It was indecent, all the more because I owed him and you my life. And now I owe it to you again. I am ashamed of myself, and deeply sorry."

She bowed her head. "I said to you once, if someone else's ways are strange to you, yours will be strange to them. Then I forgot all about that. Now I have seen something of Roman ways. They are strange to me, but I also was wrong to speak of them without respect. I understand better now. And I manipulated you, and Obala too. I owe you both an apology in return. I shall ask his forgiveness. I ask yours now."

Again, silence between them. Finally, Marcus stirred,

lifting his good hand from the cover. "Well, that's one apology apiece. Is that a fair trade, do you think?"

She looked back at him and smiled. She could hear her father's voice. "Very fair," she said. "Everyone profits." And she went back to watching the moving sea.

Glossary of Nautical Terms

after: Relatively closer to the rear of the ship.

aftercabin: Cabin at the rear of the ship.

afterdeck: A partial extra deck at the rear of the ship. *Heron* has only one afterdeck, but large ships might have two or more.

amidships: Halfway along or halfway across the ship, or both.

anchor cable: The heavy rope attached to the anchor through the anchor ring.

bale: A large pack of cloth or other goods, sewn into burlap and strapped up.

batten: A length of timber, planed flat on at least one side.

bilgewater: Stagnant water that seeps into the hull.

bitts: A heavy timber frame for securing ropes at the base of the mast.

boarding bridge: A wooden structure, more than a single plank, for crossing from one ship to another.

bolt-hole: A hole in a timber through which rope is led to secure the timber.

bow: The foremost part of the ship, sometimes called the "sharp end."

bowshot: The distance an archer might shoot an arrow.

broach-to: To be driven under water by the force of the seas, as opposed to capsizing, which is to be blown over.

bulk carrier: A broad, slow-moving ship suitable for bulk cargoes like grain, timber, or base metals.

bulkhead: A partial or full partition of timbers built across a hull to reinforce it.

catted: To secure the anchor by attaching it to a "cathead," a stub of timber projecting from the ship's side at the bow.

cross load: To load cargo while simultaneously unloading other cargo.

cross-deck: Planking nailed across beams to provide a platform.

cutwater: The point at which the ship's bow parts the water.

deck beam: A timber that supports the deck planking from below.

deck head: The ceiling of an internal compartment.

demurrage: Charges levied for using a port's facilities, like docks or cranes, longer than expected.

downwind: Toward the direction in which the wind is blowing.

embayed: Caught within an indentation of the coast. A problem if the wind is blowing towards the coast.

fairway: The channel used by ships entering and leaving ports.

forepeak: A triangular space in the hold closest to the bow.

foredeck: A partial extra deck at the front of the ship.

fother: To thread rope fibres through sailcloth, then use the resulting mat to temporarily plug a hole in the ship.

gangway: The space at a ship's side where people can board or disembark.

grapnel: Three large iron hooks bound together. When attached to a rope, thrown over a rail, and hauled in, one of the hooks will catch on the rail.

handspike: An iron bar, up to six feet long, with a point at one end.

heeling: Occurs when a ship leans over to the force of the wind. Not dangerous, unless extreme.

hold: The cargo space of a ship.

hove-to: Holding the ship in position by keeping the sail steady so that the force of the wind against the sail opposes the leeway.

hull: The frame or body of a ship.

lading, bill of: A document that lists a ship's full cargo.

leading marks: Known points on shore, such as peaks or permanent markers, which navigators can use as "pointers" to the safe channel.

leading wind: Wind blowing in a favorable direction.

leeward: The side opposite to the wind. To face to leeward is to have the wind at your back.

lee side: The side of the ship that the wind is blowing away from; opposite the weather side.

leeway: The natural tendency of all ships to go sideways when the wind blows across them. The less leeway a ship makes, the better.

lighter: A flat-bottomed harbor boat used for transferring cargo.

mainsail: The lowest and largest sail on the ship's mast, or mainmast if there is more than one mast.

masthead: The top of the mast.

oar ports: Openings in a ship's side for oars. In rough seas, oar ports were closed with leather flaps.

port side: The left side of the ship, if you're facing forward.

quarterdeck: A deck covering the rear quarter of the ship, above the main deck.

scuttle: A small opening in the hull used for ejecting waste into the sea.

sea room: Space to maneuver without running into land, especially on the lee side.

shallow draft: Able to float in a small depth of water. A vessel with a shallow draft has little wind resistance and makes much leeway.

spar: A long timber, round and tapered at one or both ends, used in the rigging of a ship.

starboard side: The right side of a ship, if you're facing forward.

stay: A rope led from the bow to the masthead in order to support the mast as well as a triangular sail called a staysail.

stern cabin: A cabin in the space below the upper deck at the stern of the ship.

tholes: Brackets for oars on the upper deck of a ship, rather than openings in the hull. See **oar ports**.

tillerman: The sailor controlling the ship's tiller, which turns its rudder.

topman: A sailor who specialized in working high in the rigging, chosen for nimbleness and light weight.

topmast: A second length of spar adding to the height of a mast. Few ancient ships had this piece of timber, but *Heron* does.

topsail: A smaller square sail, set above the mainsail.

topweight: Any weight above the waterline. The more there is, the less stable the ship becomes, so it must be kept as small as possible.

tremiolia: A type of galley, an oared ship used by the Rhodean navy. It had two rows of oars, but also carried effective sail. The design was only a limited success.

wear ship: To turn a ship around so that its bow moves away from the wind, as opposed to "tacking," or turning so that the bow moves toward the wind—a much harder task.

weather: Closest to the direction of the wind, or facing into the wind, as opposed to leeward.

windage: The estimated allowance made for the effect of the wind when setting a course. The more factors involved, the less reliable this estimate gets. Unreliable estimates in setting courses can have fatal outcomes.

windward: The side that the wind is blowing on, as opposed to leeward.

yard: A length of timber from which a sail is hung. The mainyard, from which the mainsail is hung, is a long, heavy timber.